SPELLS

COUNTERPOINT
Berkeley

A NOVEL
WITHIN
PHOTOGRAPHS

SPELLS

Peter Rock

LIBRARY OF CONGRESS CATALOGING-IN-PUBLICATION DATA IS AVAILABLE.
ISBN 978-1-61902-900-2

Book design by Afternoon Inc.

COUNTERPOINT
2560 Ninth Street, Suite 318
Berkeley, CA 94710
www.counterpointpress.com

DISTRIBUTED BY PUBLISHERS GROUP WEST

Printed in China

10 9 8 7 6 5 4 3 2 1

Sophia Borazanian

Sara Lafleur-Vetter

Peter Earl McCollough

Shaena Mallett

Colleen Plumb

Contents

A PREFACE OF A SORT

Twenty years ago, I had a job as a security guard in an art museum. This museum had five floors and a basement, a guard on every floor. The way the schedule worked was that we shifted down one floor every half hour. I started on the fifth floor, in Asian Art, then the guard who was on break in the basement came up and I moved down a floor. It was a relatively easy job, in that on a perfect day nothing changed, nothing was supposed to happen. However, boredom and loneliness kept turnover among the guards surprisingly high.

I entertained myself by trying to make up a story for each photograph, painting and object in the museum; however, we guards weren't allowed to write, on the job. Bending this rule, I carried a scrap of paper and a little pencil and then, in the minute or so when I was going down the stairway to the next floor, I'd furtively scribble a few words, to remind me of the stories I'd made up in my head. And then when I got to the break room in the basement, I'd write down as much as I could, in that half hour, then begin again. Later, I'd go home and work some more on it all.

A few years ago, I found myself in conversation with a photographer. Some of the difficult artistic questions he asked caused me to reflect on where I was with my work, and where I'd been, and reminded me of some of the pleasures and play that I was in danger of forgetting. In telling him about my museum guard writing, I began to envision a similar project.

First, I found photographers whose work I was drawn to, and contacted them with a very hypothetical and tentative description of what I was doing. Somewhat arbitrarily, I decided that five photographers would be a good number; I was gratified that the first five I contacted were excited to join me. Next, I let these photographers know why I was drawn to their work, noted some images I really admired, and shared some of my previous writing. I asked them to send me 20-30 photographs without telling me any contextual information; of these, I chose five images at a time, and proceeded incrementally, generating the specific stories as I went. Order, characters, linkages revealed themselves.

The images are not merely illustrations for a pre-existent story, then, but the conditions and possibilities and limitations of how the storytelling proceeded. The images came first. One way to think of it is that the stories herein, and the larger story they become, were already embedded in the photographs. Attention and intuition acted as a kind of excavation that brought them to the surface, into words.

SPELLS

To Begin
Is to Start

AN IDEA is not a thing you have. It cannot be possessed like that, like an envelope or a letter. A risk is a thing you take, and a decision is a thing you make. A decision is not so fragile, not so tenuous as a promise, though both are things you make, beginnings. Sometimes the invitation comes from another person or another animal, a bear or dog or ghost, sometimes it comes from oneself. It does not matter if an invitation comes from without or arises from within. Be still, yet ready to strike. Poised and taut. A snake has more than two hundred teeth, pointed backward to zip you up, to bite and hold you securely. Security is always a misapprehension. You can slip away, you can take a risk. Be decisive. Power ceases in the instant of repose, and the inside of you never stops, your heart circling your blood around and around right now, two thousand gallons in your lifetime. Wind blows in and out of you, across the deserts and mountains. It slams doors in the middle of the night, wakes you with a start.

Oceans

THIS IS THE WAY IN, the path into the forest and through it. The air is suddenly cooler beneath the trees, in the shadows. Alex reaches out to hold Sonja's hand; she doesn't see his hand, doesn't grasp it. He follows her, deeper, her dark silhouette.

"Snake, snake, snake," she says as they balance across the thick roots. This is a game she likes to play, to name animals in the darkness, to try to imagine or call them forth. Once they'd seen a real snake, slipping away so quickly, black against the black. Sonja says a snake can fly from branch to branch, throwing its long body in the shape of an S.

Above, now, the only sounds are the bare sticks of the branches rattling in the breeze, Alex's breathing and Sonja's, their footsteps. Through the trees, glimpses of houses, lighted windows. The people inside the houses are oblivious; they have no sense that every night is a journey, a voyage. The dark is another kind of ocean.

"I don't know if Naomi will come with us again," Sonja says, her voice a whisper.

"It wasn't the same," he says. "She made us keep our underwear on and everything. It's better, just the two of us."

All summer it's been like this. High school is over, and will they always know each other? Alex watches Sonja's thin, dark shape disappear against tree trunks, show itself again. Tonight, she wears a summer dress that swings out, then close against her. When she takes off that dress, her torso will be white. Her arms and legs will be dark from the sun. The white X across her back, from her swimsuit's straps.

"Oscar!" A voice shouts through the trees. "Come to the office. Oscar."

Alex and Sonja are only startled for a moment; they realize it's the loudspeaker outside of the warehouse, where men work all night in the fiberglass factory. Lights shine from the blacktop lot now, into the forest, casting sharp shadows. This is part of the path to the swimming pool, an interruption that Alex and Sonja have almost grown to expect.

"Elephant," she says. "How would that be?"

"Here?"

"It would come so slow, all these low branches here breaking across its forehead. It would kneel down for us, maybe it would."

"What will we do in the winter?" he says. "When it gets too cold?"

"I don't know about elephants and snow."

"I meant us," he said. "What will we do?"

"I don't know," she says. "Something, probably."

They walk. Their shoulders touch, drift apart.

"You don't like Naomi?" she says.

"I didn't say that." Alex looks up; the dark tree trunks seem like electrical poles, clustered together, wanting to rub against each other, or the masts of boats, rocking gently in a harbor. The wind in the branches, the rustle of sails.

Sticks snap, off to one side, in the bushes. Suddenly there's a panting, another person breathing, too, all around in the darkness. Then just the sound of the two of them again.

"It was a dog," Sonja says, once the silence has settled.

"Maybe a hyena," he says.

They're closer now. He can hear the hum of the pool, smell the chlorine, see the bright green leaves, how the light shines up into them.

"It wasn't just a dog," Sonja says. "It was a dog, I mean, only it didn't have a dog's head."

"It was headless?"

"No," she says. "It had a man's head, kind of bald. His mouth was open like a dog's, though. You could hear how he was panting. Its front paws were hands, too, instead of paws."

"Hands?"

"I don't know," she says. "I couldn't see his back feet very well."

At the edge of the trees, Sonja takes hold of the hem of her dress and pulls it over her head. It was the only thing she'd been wearing, and she stands there looking at Alex, her chest almost as flat as his, her dark arms and legs harder to see, her short hair that used to be long. She hooks her dress over a bush and leaves it there, hanging like a ghost.

Not far from here lives a girl whose shadow is the shadow of a bear.

Steam rises from the swimming pool, thinning out in the bright green trees, lost in the sky and stars. The only lights are the ones underwater, which are left on for some reason, even when the pool is closed, which it is now. The black metal fence, the sign with its hours that are not these hours. The sign says MOTEL GUESTS ONLY and NO LIFEGUARD ON DUTY, though there is a platform for a lifeguard with a chair on it. White plastic chairs are clustered together next to the pool, or set aside in twos or threes where motel guests had sat, had shared conversations.

"What are you doing?" Sonja says. "I'm shivering to death."

"To death?" Alex laughs, then pulls off his shoes, his socks. Shirt, shorts, underwear. His body is pale, too, in all the places he wishes were harder to see.

They step out of the shadows, the two of them, approaching the black fence, ready to climb it. The metal of the fence is cool, damp in their hands. And then there is splashing from the pool, the sound of voices.

Alex and Sonja bend down, hidden behind a chair, hands still clasping the fence. The sides of their bare legs touch. They listen.

"*Why is it so different at night?*" a girl's voice says. "*The water feels different.*"

"*Softer,*" another girl says, "*and heavier, too.*"

They laugh, and splash. Inside the steam, their faint dark shapes, their heads and arms show for a moment, slip away again.

"*We couldn't ever get caught,*" one says.

"*No one would ever understand,*" says the other.

"*How would it be,*" says the first, after a pause. She'd gone underwater, then surfaced again. "*How would it be if I cut off your head?*"

"*Bloody, and it would hurt. Could you do it really fast?*"

"*Depends on the knife or whatever. I don't know if I could do it at all. Really I'd like nothing better than to just tear your heart out through your mouth without any cutting.*"

"*What would it taste like?*"

The girls laugh, and splash, and submerge again. Alex realizes his forehead is pressed against the bars of the metal fence. He's leaning in as close as possible, to hear better. Sonja's doing the same, and they are still touching. His right leg against her left, their shoulders. He can feel how their breathing has fallen into the same rhythm. Above the pool, the thick green trees change shape in the wind, pulling in and letting out, as if they're breathing, too.

"It sounds like you," Alex says to Sonja.

"No," she says. "More like Naomi."

"The other one."

"Shh," she says.

The girls are talking again.

"*Let's trade names.*"

"*Clothes, at least.*"

"*Does it hurt to drown?*"

"*A little, probably. I heard freezing to death is the best. You just fall asleep. Drowning is second best.*"

"*You cough?*"

"*Your lungs fill up. You cough air out and breathe water in—*"

"*What do you see?*"

"*I don't know. That's really the question, you're right.*"

Now Sonja stands, Alex's body suddenly cold along his thigh where their skin had been pressed together. She pulls herself up on the fence, her bare foot almost kicking him in the face. She lands on the other side, twisting to look back.

"Wait," he says.

"Why?" She smiles.

He is after her, over, across the concrete to the water's edge. They pause, then leap through the steam, the voices around them, the words unclear and broken up.

Everything is blue, his eyes open, underwater, the coolness everywhere on his skin. He surfaces, gasps, goes under again, into the silence. He slips close to the round, glowing lights, their smooth surface, their faint heat. Fingers coil around his ankle, let loose.

Surfacing, he holds his arms out wide. Is he alone? He goes down again, pulling himself across, along the bottom, eyes stinging. It is a small pool, and four bodies should crowd it. Where are they? He swims to the stairs, pulls himself up.

Sonja is already there, looking down at him, into the pool. Water drips from her slippery head, onto her pale face.

"Where are they?" he says. "Did they go somewhere?"

"I can't tell," she says. "Here. Someone's coming."

Quickly they climb back over the fence, out of the light, into the shadows again, under the trees.

After a moment, a man in a motel uniform appears. He pauses when he sees the two pairs of wet footprints, running between the pool and the fence. He follows the footprints to the fence and leans against it, shielding his eyes and squinting as he tries to see into the shadows beneath the trees. He can't see anything.

Turning, he walks back around the pool, takes out his thick ring of keys, unlocks the door to the storage closet. He hits the switch for the pool lights and everything goes dark.

Alex and Sonja stumble, pulling on their clothes as they slip further into the forest.

"That was so great!" she says, her whisper tearing the darkness. "Do you feel how I feel?"

Alex is trying to keep up. He wears one shoe, carries the other.

"I think so," he said. "What happened—"

"Don't," she says, gasping, slowing to a walk. "Don't start explaining."

"I'm not."

"That was so great," she says. "I'm not even cold, and I can't stop shivering."

Guillotine

NAOMI IS ALONE in the house, and yet it is crowded by her grand-mother's broken-down, left behind things. Woodwork gouged by the old lady's wheelchair, cracks in the walls and ceilings and wallpaper, cracks in the concrete floor in the cellar. Cracks that are sounds—a sudden shift in the wood behind the walls, as if someone were walk-ing along the rooftop.

Nineteen years old, Naomi is staying in the house for as long as she wants to, maybe. For a while, out here on the edge of the forest.

In the upstairs bedroom tonight, sleepless, she opens a dresser, pulls out an old blue nightgown. Her dead grandmother's nightgown. She takes off her own clothes, pulls the nightgown over her head. It's all frayed, soft and smooth; pale blue, a strip of lace just above her breasts, that strip a little scratchy when she moves.

An old mirror leans against the wall, its white frame painted over, the stiff white petals of roses. Reflected there, Naomi sees how the nightgown's collar flops open, her pale throat. Her arms are pale, too. She stands so the mirror frames her body, so her head does not show. Cut off.

GUILLOTINE

The edge of the mirror has its own border, about an inch where the reflection is thicker, shinier, blurrier. It looks like a blade.

A guillotine, she thinks, straight across my neck, and she remembers a story she heard:

> A young woman devised a plan to make a man fall in love with her. She wore her prettiest clothes, sang beautiful songs, walked out in the moonlight, hoping to encounter him. Her strategy worked, and they became lovers, unspooling their hours together, planning and hoping. And then one night when the two of them were out walking, the young woman took a sharp knife and cut off the man's head. She wrapped the head in a sack made from her skirt and carried it down a path, through the trees, in hopes of throwing it into the river. As she walked, the head suddenly spoke to her: *You sure played a trick on me,* it said. *I knew you were smart.*

Naomi feels the heat in her underarms, the prickle along her hairline. Everything feels different with her grandmother gone, the atmosphere shifting. Her grandmother had so many stories; she was the one who told her the story of the girl and the knife, the one who could read palms and tea leaves, who tried to forecast the weather by throwing chicken bones across the cellar floor. The cellar is a dark place that Naomi, her pale blue body headless in the mirror, doesn't want to think about now.

And then, outside, a man's voice suddenly shouts:

"Why did you choose me?"

The shouting comes from below, on the street in front of the house.

"What are you doing to me?"

The upstairs bedroom is the only room with lights on. The window is behind her, off to the side. If the man can see her from the street, he can only see the mirror, her reflection.

Naomi steps sideways, through the door and into the hallway. She goes down the stairs, across the dark living room. She feels so naked in the old nightgown; she is naked beneath it.

"Just show me your face!" the man shouts. "Then maybe I'll be all right."

At the window, she wraps the dusty curtains around herself. She almost sneezes; she does not sneeze. When she looks out, the man is pacing up and down the street, still shouting, his hands up and cutting into the darkness around his head. He stares up at the bedroom window, he walks under the streetlamps, out of their light. Wearing a black suit, his hair slicked back, his heavy shoes echoing on the street.

She leans against the window; fascinated, not afraid. The man must be twice as old as Naomi, older than that. She has never seen him before.

She heard the knives in the knife drawer, sharpening each other, having their conversations.

Watching him, she becomes afraid to touch her head. It seems to her that she is looking down at him, from the angle of the upstairs bedroom—yet she knows she has come downstairs, that she must have brought her eyes, her head with her.

"Do I deserve this?" the man shouts. "Do I? Why did you choose me? Help me!"

He begins to tear at his clothes, to scratch at his face, to crawl across the blacktop. Into the round circles of light, then out of them. He moves faster, his clothes torn off, he twists his head to bite at his shoulder. It is hard to see, and his words are breaking up, into snarls. He circles in a frenzy, after his own tail, then straightens out and begins to run away, down the street, bounding, on all fours.

She watches him—a black dog in the night, heading toward the tall, dark trees of the forest—as he grows smaller, crossing beneath another streetlamp, lost in the blackness.

Out in front of her grandmother's house, the man's torn clothes are strewn in every direction, collapsed into ragged black puddles.

Four Chambers Has
the Human Heart

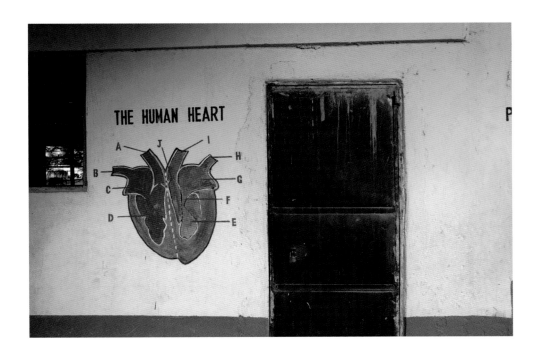

ONCE THERE WAS A GIRL who couldn't sleep. Late at night, she pulled the skins from her bed, stepped over her sleeping sister, and left her hut.

The sky was cold and black, punctured by stars. As the girl walked, she felt a knocking, as if someone was rapping on the soles of her feet from underneath the ground. She bent down and pressed her ear to the short frozen grass. What she heard was a slow beating, perhaps a distant train. She held her breath. It had to be her heart, she decided, her own heart.

Standing, she walked again. There were no trees in the night, nothing growing in any direction. Behind her, she could no longer see the fires of her village. She listened, she got down on her knees and pressed her ear to the ground once again. The heartbeat, she realized, was not her own. She decided to walk in the direction where it grew stronger.

After a time the girl was crossing a windswept plain. She approached a pile of rocks, round stones the size of a man's head. And as she began to walk around these rocks, a voice suddenly called out to her:

"Girl. Stop for a moment. Talk to me. Listen."

The stones were dark gray, the spaces between them quite black. The girl leaned close, then, and finally found a space where she could see a man's mouth. He seemed to be lying on his side, buried beneath all the heavy stones.

"Hello there," she said. "Is that your heart I'm hearing?"

"I would like to tell you a story," he said.

"You want me to help get you out?" she said.

"This is where I belong," he said. "I don't want you to get me out." His lips, framed by the sharp stones, were cracked and dark, his teeth chipped and jagged. "Was it that you couldn't sleep?" he said. "Is that how you found me?"

"I'm out walking," she said. "In my village, everyone is asleep."

"Are you lonely?" he said.

The cold wind blew across the plain, whistled on all the edges of the stones.

"Are you a dead person?" she said.

The man in the pile of stones was silent for a moment, and then he spoke again.

"I found my wife in the garden," he said, "where she'd been picking beans, leaning over the plants. A snake leapt up and bit her in the neck. When I found her, her fingers were still tight around that snake, just below his head. Both of them were dead, and on the ground was a half-full metal bowl of beans."

"Is that an answer to my question?" she said.

"If a person isn't lonely," he said, "would that person miss being lonely?"

"Is this a riddle?"

"Have you ever felt that your rib cage had been scraped clean?" he said.

"I don't think so," she said. "No, I have not."

———

The hope in this situation is that the right letters can be put together. Letters fit together can become a word, which can become a key, a key that can unlock the lock on the heavy, black metal door. When the door is unlocked, when you step inside, a wind blows the door shut. The wind, it is a thick kind of wind; it holds you where you are, and it buffets you, pulls at your clothing. The roots of your hair begin to sting. The chamber is so dark, so black that you can't tell if your eyes are open or closed, and that wind blows so hard that it pulls shadows loose from bodies, slides them away, folds them into the darkness. You have no shadow, now. It is somewhere else, doing whatever it wants to do. As you stand there, the chamber seems to expand, wind circling, roaring around you, and then the space tightens, the air sucked away so that it's difficult to breathe, to catch your breath. Your chest is tight, a chamber inside this chamber. It is said that there are four chambers, that there are two ways in and two ways out, but with the wind blowing you can't go out an in door or in an out door. And in this darkness it's impossible to guess how the other three chambers would ever be found. It's impossible to know if the key you used to access this chamber would also open those doors.

———

The sound of a girl on a bicycle with no brakes: a long slithering, all the way down a steep hill, as she drags one foot along the pavement.

———

Long ago there was a man who walked across the land carrying a sack that was cinched tight. He never let anyone look inside it. But along came a huge ice bear who was very curious.

"What's in your sack?" he asked the man.

"Nothing," the man said. "Just a big load of shit."

"Why are you carrying it around?"

"Just in case," the man said. "Just in case I need it."

This did not satisfy the ice bear, so he began to sing. His voice twisted and smoothed the air, and he sang the man to sleep.

Once the man was asleep, the bear opened the sack. Out came the wind. It untangled itself, knocked the ice bear down, and sped away in every direction. It rolled the sleeping man along the ground, quite a distance away, until he woke up.

He angrily went back to where the ice bear stood, holding the empty sack.

"Oh, traveler," the bear said. "My cave is just beyond that pile of stones, and my wife is inside. You can have my wife for a full month if you'll only get rid of this wind!"

"It's too late," the man said, hardly able to stay on his feet. "Not even a full year would be enough. Wind has entered the world."

Go-Between

ALEX AND NAOMI sat on a bench, their backs against the picnic table; she kept turning around—away from the river, away from the bridge and the cars sliding overhead—to watch the dogs in the park. The dogs were all shapes and sizes, all colors. Black and white, brown and gray, they sniffed each other, growled, ran here and there, their paths crisscrossing.

"The way their legs work," Naomi said. "How their bodies are fit together. Look."

"The dogs?" Alex said.

"Sorry," she said, turning toward him.

"Why?"

"You said you wanted to talk."

That was true. He had called her, asked what she was doing this afternoon.

"How's your grandma's house?" he said. "Is it creepy, at all, living there?"

"I don't know. It's nice having all her old things, I guess, but I keep thinking she'll be in the kitchen or she'll come down the hallway."

Two long yellow kayaks slipped past, out on the river. A lady in a bright red hat, a man with a gray beard. Naomi waved, and the man lifted his oar.

"Where's Sonja?" Alex said. "I mean, have you seen her?"

"We had breakfast this morning. Is she what you wanted to talk about?"

Off to the right was a tangle of bushes and trees, some of them tipping over into the water. Hidden on the other side of those trees, down the river, was an amusement park. Screams rose up every minute or so, every time the people on the roller coaster made the big drop, headed into the loop.

"I've known Sonja since second grade," Alex said, "like almost fifteen years, so I can't tell how things would change between us, start being a different way. It's just weird."

"But you want them to be a different way," Naomi said.

"Obviously."

"What does she think?"

Behind them, people were shouting dogs' names. Buster, Sally, Jonah.

"Did she say anything to you?" he said. "About me, I mean."

"Not really."

"It's just," he said, "we hang out together all the time, and we swim at night—"

"That's like a tradition, now."

"Yeah," he said, "but is it normal to take off our clothes to swim and then just put our clothes back on and pretend we weren't naked together at all?"

"For nothing more to happen, you mean?"

"I guess so."

"I don't know what normal is," Naomi said, after a moment. "I just figured you two knew what you were doing, or you talked about it—"

"That's not the kind of thing she talks about," he said. "Or maybe she does, to you. She talks about you all the time. I don't really know how it is, with you and her."

In the silence, three dogs—one spotted, two brown—ran around the picnic table. A wave of screams, again, came through the trees.

"I have to go." Naomi got out her phone, checked the time.

"Are you meeting Sonja?"

"No. Have to pick up my brother from school."

Alex watched Naomi walk away, the laces of her Converse trailing behind her. Then he looked up at the cars on the bridge. Red, blue, blue, silver. He gazed down along the bridge's girders to the river, to a sailboat sliding past. And suddenly, off to the right, the bushes began shaking, as if a stray blast of wind had become tangled in them.

A man's pale face stared out from the green leaves, and then his body stepped through. Thirty feet away, he wore a black suit, a white shirt, scuffed black shoes. His tie was loosely knotted, his sparse dark hair slicked back across his balding head. He moved closer to the picnic table, one hand up, pointing at Alex as he approached. His thick eyeglasses flashed like mirrors, hiding his eyes for a moment, and then there they were, dark, staring through.

"Good afternoon, young fellow," he said.

"Hi." Alex kept facing the river, expecting the man to pass by, but he did not.

"I saw you," the man said. "I watched you, sitting here with your girl, talking."

"She—" Alex said.

"I only," the man said. "I only wanted to tell you something."

"I was about to leave."

The man sat down, on the same side of the table, at the end of the bench, where Naomi had been sitting. He took out a folded white handkerchief and wiped perspiration from his high, creased forehead, from the back of his neck.

"Your girl," he said, turning to face Alex. "She's really beautiful, isn't she? I know, I know, you don't like me saying so, that makes you uncomfortable, but I just wanted to say so. You must be very happy.

I wanted to talk to someone who was happy. I'm a widower, you see, things are changing for me, I've been cut loose and I have nowhere to be."

Alex didn't interrupt. To correct the man would only encourage him. There was something—a feather, a few feathers—on the shoulder and lapel of his jacket. A plastic bag rested next to him on the bench; transparent, it seemed to be full of breadcrumbs. The man's hand trembled as he gestured, speaking.

"To tell you the truth," he was saying, "I've been following her all day. I've been thinking of her for a while. I wanted to tell her this, but then I couldn't approach her, couldn't quite do it. I didn't think I'd be able to speak the words. Do you understand?"

"You wanted to tell her that she's beautiful?"

"No, no, not that—that's no secret. What I wanted to tell her was that I had a dream about her, weeks ago, before I ever saw her. Will you tell her that, for me?"

Alex kept staring out at the river, uncertain whether or how to reply.

"Of course that would depend on the dream," the man said, quickly. "I understand that. And a dream casts shadows into the day, don't you think? I dreamed of her and then I saw her, walking down the sidewalk. May I please tell you what happened?"

Alex nodded; it seemed as if he had no choice.

"In the dream," the man began, "the girl was sleeping. That's all, really, only she looked so beautiful, in a white shirt and black tights, curled up on a bed with a red cover beneath her. Her feet were bare, and her arm was bare, her hand folded up so her fingers covered her mouth." The man held up his hand, black hairs along the back of it, to demonstrate.

"She was sleeping on her side, facing me, her eyes closed. Behind her on the bed was a camera, and a backpack, and a suitcase. The wall was wooden paneling and I just walked right through that room. I could've touched her, but I didn't. I was so close. I didn't want to wake her. I just stood there, leaning close, watching her sleep."

It was silent for a moment, only the dogs barking and their owners shouting. The man had finished talking. Alex stood and began to turn away.

"Will you please tell her?" The man stepped closer, his large teeth yellow and crooked.

"I don't know."

"I'd like to tell you another secret," the man said. "If you'd oblige. I didn't know if I would tell you this, but now I think it would be for the best. It won't take long."

Alex thought he'd begun to step away, but his legs had not moved.

"No one else knows this," the man said. "It's something I did, just the other day." Now he held out a metal bottle opener, a folded slip of paper.

Alex took the paper, unfolded it; it was a shopping list:

GARLIC
RAISINS
MILK
CEREAL

"I took those," the man said. "I thought it would make me feel better, having something of hers, but I was wrong. It only made me feel worse. Like some kind of thief."

"What?"

"These things belong to your girl. Would you please return them to her?"

"Naomi?"

"I've wondered about her name," the man said. "That's a nice thing to have. A nice name, too."

"Wait—"

"I've been telling you this. Have you been listening? She came into my dream, and so I started following her, because that was what I was supposed to do, that's how it seemed."

Alex folded up the paper and put it in his pocket. He was still standing, and now the man stood and stepped even closer, his shadow falling across Alex's face, his voice barely a whisper.

"I followed her, just the other day, to the house where she lives. She didn't know. She didn't look back. I waited on her front porch, and then I opened the door. Yes, I went inside. Through the living room, past a wheelchair, into the kitchen. I could hear her singing, I could hear the screen door open and then slap shut. I stood there, and then I saw where she was, on the back deck—but I could only see her legs! Her knees bent over the railing, her bare legs and the hem of her shorts. I took the bottle opener from the counter, and the note, that list.

"There was a glass, the print of her lips on the rim, a half inch of orange juice left and a carton on the counter. I poured myself some, drank it down. I was so much thirstier than I expected, and it was so sweet and cold! She was still singing, you understand; I couldn't tell the words. There was the sound of something dropping, when I looked up, out the screen door, I saw that her feet were bare, that she'd kicked off her sneakers.

"I stepped closer, so I could look down through the door and see her body, her arms stretched out wide, her beautiful face turned up with its black hair around it, her eyes closed. She was humming, actually, a tune I didn't know. I watched her, and then I turned and walked out through the kitchen, back through the living room, out the front door, back the way I came."

"And that was all?" Alex said.

"What?"

"That was all you did?"

"No," the man said. "You're quite right. Thank you for reminding me. Because in that moment, standing at the screen door, I wanted to talk to her, I wanted to tell her about the dream that I've now told you about, so you can tell her. But I couldn't say the words. I didn't want to startle her, and the words wouldn't come. So I found a picture—a slide, actually, a transparency—just a picture I had; I slipped it into the frame of the screen door, where she might find it, so she might know someone had been drawn to her."

Now the man stepped back, picked up his bag of breadcrumbs, and turned away. He looked over his shoulder only once as he headed toward the bushes.

"Tell her about the dream," he said.

Alex stood there, watching as the man fought his way back into the green bushes and disappeared. And then the day sped up again, the dogs barking, the sun slipping out from the clouds.

He took out his phone and called Naomi, but she didn't answer. Next, he called Sonja.

"What's up?" she said. "Missing me?"

"Something happened," he said.

"That's pretty vague."

"Something I need to tell Naomi about. Do you know where she is?"

"At the zoo with her brother, I think. I was going to meet her at her house, in a little while. Come over and walk with me."

Alex hung up the phone and looked around. It felt like someone was watching him. A small white dog chased a ball into the bushes where the man had gone; in a moment, it reappeared, tail wagging, with a bigger, black dog at its side.

———

The skirt of Sonja's yellow sundress kicked out, slapping at Alex's hand as they walked down the narrow sidewalk.

"What happened?" she said.

"Nothing, really." He liked the feeling of her wanting to know; he liked having this secret from her, something she wanted, and how she leaned close to him. "You'll hear the whole thing," he said, "when I tell Naomi."

Naomi's grandmother had died in the spring, and now it was summer. Naomi was living in the house until her parents figured out whether to sell it. They were afraid squatters would move in if it was unoccupied, since it was so close against the forest. Still, Naomi never locked the doors.

Alex and Sonja went up the steps onto the front porch and in through the door without knocking. Naomi was stretched out, napping on the couch. When they looked down at her, she opened her eyes. She smiled.

"Alex has something he needs to tell you," Sonja said. "It's a secret."

"Really?" Naomi swung her legs to the side, her feet on the floor, making room as Sonja climbed over the back of the couch.

Alex crossed to sit in the wheelchair, which sat in the corner—the three of them often practiced with it, made up games and timed themselves going room to room. He rolled himself around to face them. On the coffee table between them rested a glass half full of orange juice, next to a book of dog breeds.

"So?" Naomi said. She wore jeans and a white hoodie, her black hair in her face. The couch cushions slumped down so she and Sonja were caught in the middle, pressed against each other; Naomi lifted her right leg and put it over Sonja's left.

"So," Alex said. "Something happened at the dog park, after you left." He kept his hands on the wheelchair's rubber wheels, turning a little from side to side as he spoke. "This man in a suit came out of the bushes and talked to me."

"What kind of suit?" Naomi said.

"With a tie," he said, "only it was all a little ragged. He wasn't an old man, but he wasn't young. He was unable to approach you—that's what he said. That's why he talked to me."

"And?" Sonja said.

"He told me he had a dream about you."

"Me?" Naomi said.

"Yes."

"A dark suit?" she said. "What was I doing?"

"When?"

"In the dream."

"Sleeping," Alex said. "Sleeping on a red bed, wearing black tights and a white shirt, and your hand was twisted up like this, your fingers covering your mouth." He tried to show her. "You were sleeping, and he walked through the room."

"What did I do?"

"Nothing. You didn't wake up; you just slept."

Alex paused, thinking how he wanted to tell it, how much he wanted to say. He didn't want to tell it too fast, to waste their attention. He glanced toward the kitchen, through the doorway, the counter visible. A crack in the paint crossed the wood frame of the doorway and climbed across the plaster of the ceiling, forked along the stairway, into the shadows of the second floor above.

"Alex," Sonja said.

"The thing of it was," he said, "the man said he dreamed about you, and then later he saw you and recognized you from his dream. That's when he started following you."

Outside, a dog started barking. It got louder, as if it were close, in the front yard; gradually it faded away, down the street.

"He knows that you live here," Alex said. "I think he's followed you for a while. That's why he was watching you from the bushes."

"Creepy," Sonja said. "How excellent."

"Is someone upstairs?" Alex said. "I heard something."

"Justin," Naomi said. "He's doing his homework, I think, some project about elephants at the zoo." She looked toward the stairs, then back to Alex. "What else did the man say?"

"He told me that he came inside one day, into this house. He drank a glass of orange juice, and he took a shopping list, and a bottle opener." Standing, Alex pulled the bottle opener and the note from his pocket, handed them to Naomi.

As she read the note, he went into the kitchen. He opened the wooden door to the back deck; at first he didn't see the picture, the slide, and then he did; he pulled it loose, held it up to the light: a little girl with her shirt off, a necklace around her neck, her long hair pulled back. In a bowl next to her, bulbs were growing, stalks without flowers yet, sticking into the air.

"What are you doing?" Sonja called. "Checking the raisin supply?"

When he handed her the slide, Naomi switched on a lamp, swung the shade around. She and Sonja squinted, their heads pressed close, their darker and lighter hair mixed together. They were quiet for a moment, concentrating.

"Did I give this to you?" Sonja said.

"What?" Naomi said.

"I didn't think so." Sonja looked up at Alex. "How did you get this?"

"The man left it," he said.

"This is me," Sonja said. "From when I was a girl. I remember that time. I do. And that necklace is amber—I still have it."

"You were so cute," Naomi said, her face close to the light. "Your eyes are closed."

Alex sat in the wheelchair again, watching them. Sonja reached out, gently tucked a strand of Naomi's hair behind her ear, left that hand on the back of Naomi's neck.

"Only I don't remember anyone taking the picture," Sonja said. "I didn't know anyone was there." She looked at Alex. "Where'd you get this?"

"The man told me he put it there, wedged in the screen door."

"The man," Naomi said.

"Yes," Alex said. "He came right in and left it."

"That doesn't make any sense," Sonja said.

"We should call someone," Alex said. "Do you think we should call someone?"

"Are you afraid?" Sonja said.

"Me?" Alex said.

"Not really," Naomi said. "You said he didn't even dare to talk to me, right?"

"I don't know," Alex said. "Still—he's followed you, he knows this house."

"I'll stay here, tonight," Sonja said. "If anything happens, I'll be here."

"It'll be fine," Naomi said. "I can't tell what's happening, but I wouldn't say I'm afraid. It's just different. Everything feels different since my grandma died."

Naomi and Sonja were all entwined again, whispering words Alex couldn't hear. Slowly, he stood and stepped toward the door; he waited for them to notice, to call out after him, to say he shouldn't leave.

He listened hard, but their voices only grew softer as he went out the door, across the porch and out the steps, onto the sidewalk. He turned once—the trees in back stretched over the house, branches scratching at the rooftop—and then walked away from Naomi's house, where she and Sonja were still talking to each other, still oblivious to whether or not he was even in the room.

Reassurance

IN THE PLACE WHERE I LIVE, there are beings known as shadow people. They are known by this name because they can take the shapes of people and they are dark and slide from here to there as a shadow might. This is only to say that they can hide in a shadow and then be there all at once, the shape of a person sharp against a white wall, sliding along a sunny sidewalk, swallowed by the depths of a mirror.

These faces, they are silent. And the faces are not all that I see. In the black water, I see bears. They glow, they swim far below the surface.

Once I heard a man, the captain of a sailing vessel, assert that these beings are simply ghosts that are black, not white. Most would say that that is a simplification, a misapprehension. It is true, however, that you can't see through them—even if their edges are never quite still, always shifting, even if people say all manner of things. Not far from here lives a girl whose shadow is the shadow of a bear. That's what some say; others speak of a woman who attached her shadow to her body using a needle and thread, who pierced her skin with barbed fishhooks.

Sometimes a shadow will stay close to a person and you think it's your shadow—then its arm doesn't follow your arm, or it might get all the way loose and detached, sliding away all on its own. A shadow person can slip along the edge of a room, into any dark space, hide in a black puddle or beneath almost anything. They wait, and then when they want to they find their shape again and spill outward at various speeds.

Yet is it actually correct to link each shadow to a person, to a body, such that it might be said that one casts or causes the other? To believe this would certainly be reassuring.

Just now I was boiling mussels over the fire and a shadow twisted loose, out from under where the dogs were sleeping, right there—it shot along the stones of the beach, long and thin and then bunched up before it stretched again. An arm, another; long black fingers straight as knives. It raced into the sea, disappeared into that greater darkness.

Winged Mind

Oscar had been out wandering, passing the hours. Each morning he packed his lunch—made his sandwich, filled his thermos, cut carrots into sharp sticks—and then walked through the neighborhoods. He did not rush himself. He took care to pay attention.

He'd been leaning against a gate, in front of an apartment building with wide yellow walls. The walls were marked by a grid of windows, cut by the diagonal stairs of a fire escape. Those yellow walls, he realized, had writing on them. High up, above the stairways and platforms of the fire escape, on the third floor. He squinted; he carried no binoculars, his glasses' prescription out of date. Still, it seemed that his name was written there, on the wall, with smaller writing beneath it. He opened the gate.

The front door of the apartment building was locked. Through the glass window he could see rows of metal mailboxes, numbers and names. He went around to the side of the building, and there he found an unlocked door, propped open with a mop, a yellow bucket on wheels. That was the first day; later he tampered with the lock, bent the metal so it could easily be forced open, so no one could tell.

That first day, he wandered the dark hallways, couldn't find the stairs at first. It took a while to know his way. A hallway led past the numbered doors, on the third floor, to a bright window. With a groan, he pulled the window up, open, and stepped through, onto the rusted metal slats of the fire escape. A flowerpot held one dead plant, a few cigarette butts. He straightened, turned.

There was writing all over the wall, here—some of it painted over and showing through, most of it in pen and even pencil. Curse words and threats, promises; names added together to equal true love always or true love forever. What he'd taken for his name was not his name; instead, it was a symbol he didn't recognize, a red circle, an O with an A inside it. Next to that was the name PATRICK. And beneath the symbol in small, faint letters he could scarcely make out:

IF IT FEELS GOOD AND IT DOESN'T HURT ANYONE, DO IT.

The sun was not so bright, a warm glow, not too hot. It was such a pleasant afternoon. Oscar checked the metal steps of the fire escape, to see if the rust would come off on his fingers, and then he sat down there in the sunlight, three floors up, and began to unwrap his lunch.

He packed it each day, even though he'd lost his job at the fiberglass factory. He'd worked in the office, not the plant, yet the white dust was still everywhere, a cough that he couldn't kick, that reminded him. There would be more work at tax time, they told him, but that was far in the future. He was an accountant, had been an accountant; he could make the numbers behave. And now he did not work with numbers, but each day he still packed his lunch as if he did. Each morning he put on his suit, his tie, his sweater vest as if he might be looking for an occupation.

That first day, the sky suddenly shifted with a chuffing sound, soft slaps in the air, then a scrabbling, a settling. A pigeon perched unsteadily on the railing of the fire escape, five feet away, watching him. She was a pretty bird, turning her head from side to side so she could watch him with one eye, then the other. The shiny feathers on her neck glinted green when she moved.

"Is it my sandwich?" he said. "Is that what you want?" He held it out, and as he did he noticed something else about the bird: attached to one leg, one ankle, was a small yellow pouch, a bag that held something inside it.

When he stood, the bird fluttered away, but she circled back. She wanted to come to him. It wasn't only the crumbs he left for her, in a line that led to the tip of his shoe. She wanted him to hold her; she wanted to pick at the sandwich as he held it, to pull out the lettuce and shake it in her beak. She pressed against him, she cooed, and he could feel the sound, the soft vibration against his chest.

Inside the pouch was a roll of paper, a tiny scroll. The message on it was typewritten; he pushed his glasses up on his forehead so that he could read it:

AND WITHOUT A HEART, A PERSON IS BENEATH
A PILE OF STONES QUITE A DISTANCE FROM HIS
FELLOW HUMAN BEINGS

Oscar took his pen from his pocket and uncapped it, thinking. Then he turned the scroll over, holding it flat against his leg, next to the pigeon, and wrote:

IF IT FEELS GOOD AND IT DOESN'T HURT ANYONE, DO IT.

He closed the pouch and lifted the pigeon back onto the railing. He watched as she dropped down before catching the air with her wings, unsteadily climbing away.

Next, Oscar stood and gathered his things. The pen still in his hand, he signed his name on the yellow wall, Oscar DiStefano, and then he went back through the window, closed it behind him, and down the hallway, back the way he'd come.

The next day, it took longer to get inside the building, but he did. And he had to wait longer for the pigeon to appear, but she did.

The other pigeons, they were not so forthcoming, right away—his friendship with the first one acted as a kind of recommendation, though, and soon they'd come to him, bring their messages. Their claws scratched his wrists as they tried to get at the bag of bread-crumbs he brought. Their wings slapped his glasses from his face and he was blind, for a moment, surrounded by sharp shadows. That second day, he received three messages, and he answered each one.

PEOPLE WHO GO MISSING AND ARE CONSIDERED
DEAD OFTEN TURN UP ALIVE IN OTHER PLACES,
MUCH LATER. PEOPLE WHO ARE LOST AT SEA
CAN EMERGE FROM ANOTHER BODY OF WATER.

I DREAM OF GROWING A LONG BEARD AND LIVING
ON THE SEASHORE SOMEWHERE. I WANT TO HEAR
THE WAVES AS I FALL ASLEEP.

WRITE ME ONE THING ABOUT YOURSELF,
AND I WILL WRITE ONE THING ABOUT MYSELF.

ISN'T THAT WHAT WE'RE DOING?

THE GIRL WITH THE FIREFLY IN HER HAIR WAS
UNAWARE THAT SHE WAS BEING SHOUTED AT,
AND SOMEONE ELSE IN THE BOAT PICKED IT OUT
FOR HER.

ARE FIREFLIES DANGEROUS TO GIRLS?

He learned that asking questions was difficult, if he expected answers. Each time the birds came they had new messages, and it was unclear where his questions had gone. When he wrote on the blank sides of each new message, he tried to reply with the same bird who had carried the message. He did not want to mix up his answers among the birds—he assumed they all returned to the same place, yet he could not be certain, and that was fine. It was a blind conversation, a conversation where one could be honest.

As he sent the birds away, he wrote down this conversation on the yellow wall next to him, before he forgot it. Then he feared it would be painted over, so he transcribed it into the end pages of the paperback he carried.

Some days he waited and the birds did not come. He sat and dozed, or read his book—Ray Bradbury stories, the pages full of breadcrumbs. There was a window just down the wall and sometimes it opened and he could hear a woman singing, the splash of water and clatter of plates as she washed them. He heard children's voices, playing somewhere, but he couldn't see any children below. Waiting, he read the names on the wall and wondered if maybe they had been here before him, receiving messages, or if one of these names was the name of the person—somewhere in the city, standing on another building's rooftop—who sent out the pigeons. This person repaired his wire coops up there, waiting to see what Oscar would say.

The pigeons, the birds came to be more than conveyances. Oscar had his favorites. He gave them names. Hazel, with her damaged foot; Impatience, who tore at the plastic bag with his beak; Isabel, who gently scratched bread crumbs from between Oscar's lips, who settled on his shoulder as if she were a parrot and he a pirate. She was the first one, on that first day.

Their feathers, both soft and sharp, sliced sounds from the still air, dusted the rusty metal of the fire escape. As he watched them swoop away with the new messages he imagined them each as a kind of winged mind, a head struggling along through the sky, wanting to find somebody to talk to, to share with.

THE HUMAN HEART IS A MUSCLE DESIGNED TO
REMAIN STRONG AND RELIABLE FOR A HUNDRED
YEARS OR MORE.

ONCE I HEARD A STORY OF FIREFLIES IN A FOREST
THAT TURNED OUT TO BE PEOPLE WITH FLASHLIGHTS
AND HEADLAMPS.

WHAT TO DO AND WITH WHOM TO DO IT?

Oscar read this, and pondered it for a long moment before he answered. The words he wrote were true, but it was still difficult to write them down:

> IN A DREAM I SAW A GIRL I'D NEVER SEEN BEFORE. SHE WAS
> SLEEPING. SHE DIDN'T SAY OR DO A THING TO ME. SHE JUST
> SLEPT THERE AND I WALKED THROUGH THE ROOM. AND THEN
> ONE DAY ON THE STREET I SAW HER WHILE I WAS AWAKE.

Time passed, and the birds' feathers lost their luster. They were disheveled, they jerked through the air like broken kites. It could have been the weather, or something else. Were the birds sick, or were they simply growing old?

Perhaps they were not being fed or cared for, perhaps something had happened to their keeper, the writer of the messages. It was impossible to know. Eventually only Isabel came, and the message she brought was always the same.

YES FIREFLIES CAN BE QUITE DANGEROUS
TO GIRLS.

He unrolled it, read it again, and replaced it, still hoping it might be delivered; he did not change his answer, on the other side:

> I HAVE PURSUED MY LIFE IN A FRIGHTENED FASHION,
> YET I HAVE NEVER BEEN MORE UNAFRAID THAN I AM NOW.

These messages, Oscar did not know if they were meant for him, or if he'd intercepted them, or if there was a difference. The birds, the messages came to him for only a month. They came to him as reassurance, as confidence and mystery. He'd found this new occupation, which was to follow his curiosity, to be open to signs and messages, all sorts of possession and shift. It was a kind of love, and he tried to be its instrument, to live under the feelings and spells that passed through him and were cast out, to understand his impulses as a kind of divining rod.

It's Not Like It's
One or the Other

NAOMI AND SONJA sat together on the grassy slope; below, the city spread out, cut in half by the dark river. The bright blue sky stretched all around them.

"My neck's sweaty," Naomi said. She braided her black hair into two thick braids, then took off her red sweater. She lay back atop her sweater and closed her eyes.

"We could call someone with a car," Sonja said. "Drive somewhere to swim."

"You and swimming," Naomi said.

The warm wind pulled at their words, their clothing. A woman further down the slope chased a white napkin, a sandwich in one hand. Pigeons hopped along a footpath.

"Any sign of the man?" Sonja said.

"I've been watching for him," Naomi said. "I've been expecting him."

Last week, their friend Alex had been at a park with Naomi; when Naomi left, a man had come out of the bushes and told Alex that he'd been following her, that she was beautiful, that he'd sneaked into the

house where she lived. The man gave Alex a bottle opener that he said came from her kitchen.

"Maybe I did see him, actually," Naomi said. "But this was before, before he talked to Alex. A man watched me, some man."

"When?" Sonja said.

"He watched me through the window—I was trying on one of my grandmother's nightgowns and he was down on the street. It probably wasn't even the same man."

"There's more than one?"

"I doubt it."

"What did he do?" Sonja said.

"Nothing, really. He ran away."

"How did it feel, to have him watch you?"

"What do you mean?"

"What if he came back?" Sonja said. "What if he had a knife or a gun or something?"

Naomi laughed. "I guess I'd have to do whatever he said."

"Alex made him sound kind of pathetic," Sonja said. "And no one else ever saw him—Alex could've just made the whole thing up. I mean, have you missed anything else?"

"No," Naomi said. "A notebook, I guess, where my brother was working on his homework, but he could have lost that a lot of places. Justin, he's always losing things."

"I wish I had a little brother."

"No, you don't."

The day felt hazy. The girls lay close, next to each other, touching at their shoulders, hips, their ankles when they shifted. The night before they'd hardly slept, naked together atop the sheets, waiting for a breeze through the window that never came. Now their fingers brushed each other's, clasped, let loose again.

"If I went away," Naomi said, her eyes still closed, "you wouldn't forget me?"

"Never."

"Would you stay in my grandmother's house, watch it?"

"Why would you go away?" Sonja said.

"It'd be free. You could get someone else to live with you. A couple people, even. There's lots of room."

"You're serious? When would you come back?"

"I don't know."

"But you will?"

"I think so."

"Why didn't you say, before?"

"I just found out," Naomi said. "Something in my grandma's will. It's a ticket, a ticket on a boat." She opened her eyes, squinted at the sky. "She wanted me to take a trip."

"I don't want you to go."

"I have to. She's dead, and she wanted me to do it."

"That's a reason?" Sonja said.

"Yes."

"Where?"

Naomi didn't answer. After a moment, she rolled onto her side. Leaning on her bent elbow, she squinted at Sonja.

"Do you really think Alex would make up a story like that?"

"Like what?"

"About the man."

"I don't know," Sonja said. "I guess I don't see why he would."

The sound of the wind was all tangled in the rush of the distant traffic. The voices below blurred together, not quite broken into words. The air felt warm, thickened; the grass smelled sweet and green.

"I'd sleep with him," Naomi said. "If that's what he wanted. If he was as into me as he's into you."

"Who? Alex?"

"Yes."

"Where's that coming from?" Sonja said.

"You wouldn't?"

"If you were you," Sonja said, "or if you were me?"

"I'm just telling you what he said."

"When? What did he say?"

"The other day. Just that he's into you and he can't tell what you think about it."

"And what did you tell him?"

"That I didn't know what you wanted," Naomi said, "how you felt about that. I said it was between the two of you."

"Don't you care?" Sonja said.

Clouds gathered and dispersed, pulled apart by the sun. Naomi rolled onto her back again, closed her eyes. She rested her hands on her belly, the flowered fabric of her dress.

"You want to," she said, a little while later. "Don't you?"

"I'd rather be with you," Sonja said. "Like last night. How it is. It's just weird—I've known Alex since we were little."

"It's not like one or the other. It's not something like that."

"Like what?"

"Like you have to be with him or be with me, like it's some kind of choice."

"That's what you say," Sonja said.

"I wish I had someone like Alex," Naomi said.

"You have me."

"But I didn't know you when you were a little girl. I wish I had that."

"I've told you stories about it. I can tell you, you can know me that way. We'll know each other for a long time, right?"

The girls were quiet for a time, lying there on the grass, beside each other with the sun shining on them. This was their afternoon. No one knew where they were. They had no place else to be.

"I think about her," Naomi said. "All the time, now. My grandmother. It's since I'm, since we're in her house, all her things around everywhere; I miss her, even though she told me not to worry. She told me she wasn't worried about dying, not at all. She'd been there, she'd seen it, and it really wasn't so different than here. She told me a whole story about it."

Sonja rolled onto her side, closer to Naomi, as she listened. Naomi's voice was sleepy, scattered by the wind. Her eyes were closed.

"My grandmother walked through a forest, deep into a forest and then out the other side, across a desert where stones were piled up, markers to follow. She walked past broken machines, abandoned buildings. Once she saw a black dog in the distance, but it disappeared before she could get close—"

Naomi's voice trailed off. It was easy to look at her, to watch her, now. No rings on her fingers, no jewelry, only a black hairband around her left wrist. The flowers on her dress were so bright; at the seam they didn't quite match up, so some of the petals seemed torn. Sonja propped herself up on one elbow, and her dark shadow fell across the bright flowers, across Naomi's hands. Reaching out, Sonja traced a finger down Naomi's bare arm. From her shoulder to her elbow, then the bend to the forearm, closer above her body, to her hand.

"What?" Naomi said.

"Does that bother you?"

"No. It feels good." Naomi didn't open her eyes, her lashes straight and black. Her black braids crossed each other, a jagged X in the green grass above her head.

"That was a crazy dream," Sonja said.

"Oh," Naomi said. "It wasn't a dream, and I didn't even finish telling it."

"Finish, then."

"So, my grandmother walked up a white path that cut back and forth, climbing a black, black hill. She'd almost reached the top of the slope stretching up away from her, and at the line, the edge of that horizon something dark rose up, just a roundness against that line. It swayed, rising, and as it emerged she realized that it was a person's head.

"Someone was climbing up the other side of the mountain, toward her. Next, a long neck was visible, then narrow shoulders, a thin arm rising up to wave. It was a man, and the way he was coming, waving like that, she thought he must recognize her. The light shone behind him so she couldn't see his face, his head still bobbing as he descended the path, as he approached her. The man looked a little like a scarecrow, and once he was close it was clear that he was not a person my grandmother knew or had ever known. He was a young man, so thin, with a large Adam's apple that trembled as he stopped before her, both of them standing on that white path."

"This wasn't a dream?" Sonja said.

"No."

"Then what was it?"

"Listen: the man was struggling to get something out of the pocket of his pants—he wore a dark suit that was much too small for him, and heavy boots. His clothes were all wet, dripping on the ground. Finally he managed to pull an envelope from his pocket, and held it out to her. She opened it, pulled a slip of paper from inside.

HELLO. I AM HAPPY TO MEET YOU AND WISH YOU WELL ON YOUR JOURNEY. I HAVE TAKEN A VOW OF SILENCE THAT I HOPE YOU WILL RESPECT.

"She read this, and wondered if she should say something. She handed back the note, and the young man smiled, the paper wet from his hand as he forced it back inside his pocket. For a moment, as my grandmother stepped aside, she believed, she hoped that he would walk beside her, that they would walk together. But he kept on in the direction she'd come from, down the hill, and once he was gone she started up the slope by herself.

"The air was shimmering around her, and as she neared the top she could hardly see her own feet. It seemed she was walking into light, that she might fall off an edge, and she was ready for that. That was when she heard wings, birds, and there were seagulls wheeling around her. All at once she saw that it was an ocean spread out, far below, reflecting the light—"

A barge moved slowly along the river, cars on the bridges. Sonja waited for a moment. Gently, then, she touched the damp nape of Naomi's neck, she kissed her bare shoulder.

"Are you asleep?" she said.

Justin N.   Room 5, Mrs. Trevithick   6th Grade

ELEPHANTS

I have chosen to write about elephants because they have larger brains than any animal and I've liked them since I was little. Elephants are vertebrates. Their backs are made of a chain of circular bones. An elephant graveyard is where old elephants go to die, far from the herd.

Elephants live in families. The oldest grandmother is in charge and has the best memory. Poachers try to shoot the oldest grandmother first so everyone else will be confused. Poachers take the elephants' tusks for pianos and jewelry. My grandmother wore jewelry, and when she died we were confused. After school I go to her house where my sister lives, now. The wheelchair is still there and I sit in it and my sister helps me with my homework like this paper about elephants.

Elephants come from wooly mammoths whose tusks fought with the long fangs of saber-toothed tigers. These tigers were carnivores. Elephants are herbivores. They are the only mammals that cannot jump. At the circus they can walk in a line with their feet on each others' backs or balance with all four feet on a very large, strong ball. They cannot climb trees or get on top of many things because nothing could hold them. They'd crash right through a house if they tried to stand on a rooftop. They could crush a person inside!

My grandmother died more slowly inside her house. When she could still walk she'd go into the basement and throw chicken bones on the floor and tell me the future. Like how I'd meet a girl who owned a snake and would know the names of the constellations.

Elephants turn over the bones in the elephant graveyard like they still know their dead friend. They lift up the bones gently like they are trying to wake up a sleeping baby. Elephants do recognize each other so they know who to trust. The grandmother remembers the most things of anyone but her memory is so long that she might make mistakes like taking the herd to a feeding place that is no longer there, that is now a place where humans live.

Humans have stronger eyesight than elephants. Even though they have large ears their hearing is poor. One of the softest parts of their body is at the back of their ears, called the knuckle, like a knuckle on your hand. Elephant trainers steer the elephant by pressing on these knuckles with their feet.

When elephant family members or friends meet after they've been apart, they trumpet and are joyous. Elephants can live to be seventy years old or even older. My grandmother died when she was 81 years old.

When I go to the zoo I spend the most time with the elephants. I watch them and try to listen to them. Elephants purr like cats to communicate. They can also grunt, bellow, whistle and trumpet.

At the zoo I have watched them stand in one place, swaying, swinging their trunks, lifting one foot and putting it down without going anywhere. They can do this for hours. This is called weaving and damages the elephants' feet and joints. It becomes difficult to get them to stop once they start. Elephants in the wild never do this. It is a bad sign and it makes me feel funny and sad to watch it. I have never been hypnotized.

Elephants are the largest land animal. Blue whales are larger, but do not live on land. Not many people know that elephants can swim long distances. They use their trunk to breathe like a snorkel when they are swimming in deep water.

Blue Water,
Blue Mountains,
Blue Sky

ALEX KICKED HIS WAY DEEPER, his bare ribs brushing the corner of something hard and square. He opened his eyes: through the brownish, reddish water he saw four black bull's-eyes, ten feet down. The burners of a stove, he realized; and the shape next to him, looming pale and silent, a refrigerator. A kitchen, he was swimming through a kitchen. He rose through the ceiling—there was no ceiling, no rooftop, all that carried away when the flood came, when the reservoir filled. Surfacing, he called out to Sonja. She was underwater somewhere, perhaps nearby in some room, or in some other house, or beneath him, in the yard. Jagged underwater trees scratched his stomach as he swam over them. It was impossible to know what all was beneath him; dark shapes twisted and folded away. Rolling onto his back, he stared into the blue sky, the wispy clouds, and then Sonja was next to him, laughing, and their friends were shouting from up the slope—next to the car, already out of the water, waiting.

That was earlier this summer, that day of swimming, the day Alex realized how it might be with Sonja. Their friends had decided to find thirteen swimming holes in one afternoon; he hadn't known Sonja was coming, hadn't seen her for a long time, and there she was. They kind of paired up, swimming, and they sat in the back seat, talking about all sorts of things. That was months ago, and tonight he is alone, skating through the city streets, kicking hard across the bridge, the river below; downtown, to skate the empty fountain. He's left his phone at home. He isn't trying to go anywhere, to find anyone.

He skates. Under a streetlamp, into the shadows, crouching lower, dragging his fingertips along the blacktop. He met Sonja in elementary school, so long ago—their parents knew each other, they still do. She'd even skated with him, back then, and in junior high; he never saw her skate, after that. Now he tries a kick-flip off a bench, his board skittering away, into the bushes; he chases it, picks it up and shakes it off, throws it onto its wheels and he's rolling again down the long hill—no traffic tonight and he slaloms the yellow lines, the dashes in the middle of the street, leaning hard into the turns, the wind in his ears. Sonja is somewhere, tonight. Maybe with her friend Naomi, up to something, whatever they do together. He doesn't know, he can't figure it out. He only has the different ways he is feeling, the feeling that the more time he spends with Sonja, the happier he will be. But now there's Naomi, suddenly more than a friend to Sonja, something more that Alex hadn't expected.

Why should he expect anything, or know how people are, anyway? And who cares how he feels? Just because you feel a certain way about someone doesn't mean they have to feel that way about you.

Swimming away from the sunken houses that day, into the shallows and out of the reddish water, Alex and Sonja found their towels, scrambled up the broken slope where the car was idling with its back door open. They were moving as soon as they climbed in, the door slamming with the acceleration and already in the front seat the others were having an argument about music. They played ten seconds of one song, ten seconds of another. Alex buckled his seatbelt. Sonja rolled down her window. They sat on top of their towels, their suits still wet, in the back seat together.

"I wonder," he said, "I wonder where the people are now, the ones who lived in that house."

Sonja took out a lollipop from the bag at her feet, offered him one. Lemon. Hers was orange, and she unwrapped it, put it in her mouth, fingers twirling the stick. The sun shone in on her side of the car, so her face was dark, a silhouette. A rubber band around her wrist, for her hair, but her hair was loose, in sharp points that dripped on her shoulders. The sun bright on her chest and her arm and her knees. Her far knee was bent up, just above the edge of the open window. Through the window, the blue water, the blue mountains on the other side, the blue sky above. There were goosebumps on Sonja's skin.

"I want adventures," she said. "Things are only beginning. It's adventures I want but I also feel different, I want to feel how I used to feel."

"How?" he said.

"Like when I was a girl," she said.

"We have the swimming pool in the forest," he reminded her, the place they swam at night, and it seemed like she was nodding but she was also looking out the window, swooping her hand up and down in the wind. She spoke, and her voice was so soft that he could barely hear it:

"When I was little," she said, "I believed I could make plants grow by thinking hard, standing close to them; I thought my moods changed the weather and not the other way around. We had a dog named Romeo—"

"Yes," he said, leaning into the space between them. "I remember that dog, a long time ago. Like second grade?"

"He died," she said, "and we made him a fancy wooden coffin, my dad did, but when we buried him I wouldn't let anyone put the lid on, so he'd be able to get out, if he wanted to. I believed that."

Out the window, a wide blue lake, mountains around it. It used to be a volcano, someone from the front seat said, it's almost bottomless, and when the car pulled over everyone leapt out, shouting, running down toward a narrow dock on the shore.

Looking into the clear water from the floating dock, no one could see the bottom. It stretched down and down and down. Like a well but not so dark; like outer space. Alex felt Sonja's hand on his arm, moving him aside.

And then she was in the air, feet pointed down. Into the blue water with hardly a splash, hardly a sound.

The top of her head, round and dark, grew smaller and smaller and smaller; Alex leaned over in the silence, watching. Just before the dark circle of her head disappeared, it began to move sideways, and then Sonja's body was stretched out, down there, a thin black shadow. It bent and twisted like an eel, her arms and legs stretching thin, almost impossible to see.

It was silent. Alex leapt.

This water was just-melted ice, squeezing his ribs, his lungs, collapsing tight around him. He kicked sideways, whipped his arms through the waves, trying to warm up. A ways from the dock already, he was treading water, spinning in every direction. The bright sun reflected off the low, sharp waves. Where was she? The surface of the water like the skin, the scales of a fish, glinting all around him. It was hard to see; he had to kick harder, to rise up and see over the waves. His feet were numb, his hands.

And then at last, farther out than he believed she could be, Sonja surfaced. Her head gently rose and fell with the movement of the shining waves.

What Is Known

ARE THEY OUT TO FRIGHTEN PEOPLE? What kind of purpose or motivation would that be? Perhaps this is a misunderstanding. Let's begin here: What do we actually know?

They're usually white, but they can be invisible, any color. The whiteness is so they can be seen in the darkness. That's all. That's usually when we're able to see one. Or more than one. They aren't always alone, they can travel together. Are they lonely, do they miss something, someone? They might hold a person inside them, digesting—they might hold a period of time, or a place, all different weather. They can, after all, be any shape they choose.

Or perhaps they don't choose, but they rarely complain. They don't malinger.

Do they haunt places, do they haunt people? That's such a strong word, thick with connotation. How do they move? You can see for yourself: all manner of ways. Quick or slow, smooth or stuttering. Sometimes the air is thick and heavy. Other times it's slippery and then nothing can be stopped, once it starts moving.

Illuminations

WALKING ALONG THE TILE-ROOFED WALL of the university, following the children's voices, Oscar approached the elementary school.
Beyond the voices, beneath them, was the sound of water. He bent
down on the empty street and pressed his ear to the round, metal
manhole cover; water rushed below, unseen—the last three days of
rain, all rushing toward the river.

Standing, he felt the night air cool on his scalp, his skull. This morning, shaving his face, he'd nicked his sideburn and then simply kept
going. With scissors he'd cut his hair down close and then shaved it
all smooth.

He walked, following the white board fence along the playground,
reluctant to part with the voices on the other side. The sunset had
been pink and orange, set off against the smoke from a fire downtown, and now the sky hung bluish black. When he turned to his left,
the fence gave way to an embankment, a dark slope. He hurried forward with short steps.

Along the top of the embankment was a bobbing cluster of beautiful
lights. Shining in the air, flickering, then dim again.

A girl shouted, another light. A boy answered: a spot of fire against
the dark blue sky.

Oscar took off his heavy eyeglasses, polished them, fit them on again, trying to understand what he was seeing. It must have happened like this: one of the neighborhood children had found this place, one night—a space on the slope where their voices lit up in the darkness, something tight in the air that made sound bright, illuminated.

Everywhere there were voices, spots of light around the dark shapes of the children—girls with long hair, in skirts, skinny boys with their sweatshirt hoods pulled up—and other lights settling in the bushes.

Oscar moved closer, along the edge of the bushes. The children didn't notice him, they were so focused on what they were doing. Now a boy—it was a boy he recognized, the one he'd been following—reached up and caught a light. He opened his clasped hands slowly.

"Look."

A girl leaned close, and in that moment both their faces were lit, close together, only inches apart. His proud smile, her bright intelligent eyes. Their two faces there in the night, then gone. Another light, winking in her dark hair, where it hung down her back; she didn't notice, and another girl picked it out.

Someone clapped their hands, and then someone else. The children were catching the small spots of light and breaking them, smearing them on their arms and legs. It wasn't long before the embankment was full of glowing skeletons, shrieking, silhouetted there.

But the glow didn't last, and the first boy began shouting. "Stop that! You're killing them!" His shouts were not lit; he ran from child to child, scolding them.

Soon, the children began to disperse, down the embankment, through the dark bushes, past Oscar without seeing him or giving him much notice. At last only the boy and girl were left, standing close together. One light blinked above their heads, and then it was gone. The night sky, the stars.

"How many more days?" the boy said.

"I don't know," the girl said. "And if I don't talk to you at school tomorrow, that doesn't mean anything."

"Okay."

The boy took one step back, held out his hand. The two children shook hands, rather formally, and then the girl turned away and walked down through the trees, her body blending into the shadows beneath them. The boy watched her go. He stood alone on the embankment, his thin, dark body against the sky. In that moment, it seemed that if he were to shout, all the darkness surrounding him would suddenly be torn to brightness.

"Justin," Oscar said, calling out, stepping from the shadows. "Justin. I have something for you."

"Who's that?" The boy sounded afraid; he took a step away, toward the streetlamps at the bottom of the embankment.

"I found your notebook," Oscar said. "Your school notebook, with your writing in it. I've been trying to return it to you."

"I lost it," the boy said. "I left it at my sister's house."

"Yes," Oscar said. "I'm a friend of Naomi's."

"She's going away, you know. On a boat."

"I didn't know that," Oscar said. "But it seems wise. Travel enriches us."

"Aren't you too old to be Naomi's friend?"

"I took this by mistake." Oscar held up the pale blue notebook, JUSTIN N. scratched into the cover with ballpoint pen. Oscar wasn't close enough to hand it to Justin; he didn't want to let go of it, not yet.

"Where?" the boy said. "How?"

A flash of light, off to the left. Oscar turned his head; nothing but darkness. Above, birds sliced through the night sky. Crows, pigeons, bats.

"I read what you wrote about elephants," Oscar said.

Now that the boy had the notebook, Oscar was nervous that he'd leave quickly, that he'd run away. But Justin still stood there, maybe five feet tall, holding the notebook by its metal spiral.

"Do you really know my sister?" he said. "I'm going to ask her."

"Who was that girl you were talking to?" Oscar lifted his hand to smooth his hair back and there was only the skin of his scalp. "Was that your girlfriend?"

"She has a snake," Justin said, at last. "Kiyoko does. But I've never been to her house so I've never seen it."

"What kind of name is that?"

"It's late," Justin said. "I was only allowed out for the fireflies."

They were silent for a moment, each gazing up into the dark blue sky around them.

When Oscar looked away from the stars, the boy was halfway down the slope, walking quickly away. He turned left, once he reached the street, and soon he was out of sight, headed home.

Oscar shuffled across the embankment, back around the white board fence. He stepped between parked cars, out into the quiet, deserted street. He tested the handles of the cars' doors until he found one that was unlocked.

An old sedan. The light in the ceiling turned on when he opened the door, as he moved quickly, his thick fingers clumsily finding the latch for the trunk, pulling it—and then he quietly closed the door, the light suddenly dark, everything still quiet.

In the trunk, Oscar pushed the spare tire aside, lifted it out of the way, then found the metal rod, the tire iron. This was what he need-ed. The trunk had no light; he left it open behind him as he turned and walked up the street, back to the manhole, the storm drain where, earlier, he had listened to the water.

The fit was not perfect, but he managed to pry the heavy cover up, to get a hand underneath it. A circle, designed to not fall through; he rolled it carefully to the gutter, leaned it there. Next, he took off his thick glasses, rubbed the bridge of his nose. He set the glasses on a bush, hooked them there for someone to find tomorrow, glinting in the morning light.

He imagined someone watching him as he turned. His smoothly shaved head, his black suit and tie, his heavy shoes. He tried not to slow, not to adjust his stride as he approached the hole, so perfectly round, pure black. One foot in and the trailing one barely snagging, his rib, an ear brushing the hard side of the hole as he fell.

Hardly time to catch his breath, all blackness, the sky closing away.

A jolt.

The cold, the pain in the bones of his legs, the water not deep, not shallow, not still. He slid rapidly, sinking not down but sideways. His body spun a little, swayed rhythmically, as though he were hesitating and, carried along by the current, bounced gently along the concrete walls, though sticks and small branches, through tangled plastic bags. Beneath the neighborhoods, through the city. Beneath a house where a family sat in their kitchen, finishing dinner, another where a lonely woman washed dishes, a girl alone in her grandmother's bedroom. Oscar didn't stop, like the flotsam around him in the darkness. A white milk jug, a swirl of cigarette butts that straightened in a line, clustered again.

Closer to the end of the tunnel, light filtered in, and sound, and Oscar's body bumped through a shallow section, was hung up on a metal grate—bent sideways, at the waist, arms stretched limply out before the water gathered up behind him and pushed him through.

He rolled, straightened again, plunged into the river, the depths. Crayfish shot away, backward, trailing their claws. Carp slid into the shadows. And then he was met by a cluster of salmon. Seeing the dark body, the fish stopped, uncertain, then suddenly turned away and disappeared. Just as suddenly, they returned swiftly to Oscar and zigzagged around him as he moved through the current, as he sank deeper, bumping along the riverbed.

After that another dark body appeared. It was a sturgeon. Longer than Oscar, heavier, it swam under the man with disinterest. It turned its whiskered shovel-nose upstream and slipped away, hovering close to the bottom of the river, moving like something prehistoric.

Overhead at this time the clouds were massed together, dark against the night blue of the sky. Headlights blinked through the railings of the bridge as cars passed across the river. The lights winked in moments, disappeared, then surfaced through the darkness in places you could not predict.

The Daughter and the Dog

THERE WAS ONCE A LARGE, BLACK DOG who was owned by a family with one small daughter. This gentle dog was a companion to the family for many years. His wagging tail slapped the kitchen cabinets. His fierce barking persuaded strangers not to linger. As the dog slept, the small daughter often slept with her head resting on his ribs. She knew well his gentle snoring, his leg twitches, the rise and fall of his body.

One day the family looked out into the yard and saw the dog sleeping in the shadow of a tree. Later in the day, he had still not moved. When the daughter went outside, she saw flies on the dog's coat and the dog not lifting his head to snap at them.

The father in the family was a carpenter, and he built the dog a wooden coffin. He dug a square grave in the yard as the daughter stood and watched. A neighbor girl from the village wandered over to see what was happening, then went to look at the dog, who still waited beneath the tree. A wool blanket rested on top of him, and when the girl lifted its edge, to see, the daughter told her to go away.

The daughter was very young and still learning to speak. She had a few words, but knew how to communicate, to make herself understood. As her father moved the dog's stiff body and fit it into the wooden coffin, the daughter refused to let him attach the coffin's lid. He tried to do it as he planned, as you would expect him to, but she would not allow it. In the end, the father had to do as she wished. He did not put the lid on the coffin. He set the dog in on his back, all four legs sticking up as the dirt was shoveled in.

The daughter in this story is a friend of mine, and that's how I know it's true. The first time she told it to me, I didn't believe her, even though she said she hadn't made it up. And every time, over the years and as I got to know her better, every time I asked her, the story came out exactly the same.

My friend, the daughter—after the dog was buried, the daughter became quite ill. She had a terrible cough, and wouldn't eat. Worst of all, she could no longer speak. It wasn't so much that she'd lost her voice, she told me, as she had lost her words.

In any case, the family tried to keep the daughter in bed, but sometimes they found her in the yard, standing next to or walking circles around the dog's grave. When they did, they brought her quickly back inside.

One day the daughter leaned down and brushed the loose dirt from the grave with her small, flat hands. Carefully, she uncovered the bottom of the dog's paws. The pads were rough, worn down, yet they were not as cold or stiff as she had expected.

The next day the family was eating breakfast together in their kitchen. Out the window the father noticed that the grave was disturbed, the dirt scattered, the earth caved in.

The dog stood in the yard, shaking dirt from his coat as if it were water and he'd been swimming, not buried underground. He moved stiffly, so strangely that the family did not approach him right away. He kept blinking his eyes, trying to get the dirt out of them, snapping his jaws, shaking his head. At last the daughter stepped closer to him. She licked her finger and cleared his eyes so that he could see.

After he surfaced, the dog no longer responded to his name. In fact, he seemed to be deaf. Also, he had lost his voice and made no sound at all. His knees didn't bend, and he lurched stiffly around the yard. It seemed he would tip over, but he never did. He never lay down. He never ate or drank that anyone saw, nor did he urinate or defecate. He was as unlike a dog as a dog could be.

However, the dog's reappearance seemed to heal the daughter. In fact, she began to speak like a much older person, using long words and saying things that the members of her family could not understand. She spoke of sea journeys and lands of ice, animals swimming in the depths, far below the surface—all manner of experiences she could never have lived.

Sometimes the daughter stood in the yard for hours, talking and talking, and the dog stood listening, silent and unsteady, his muzzle grayer than anyone could remember.

A week after he'd climbed from his grave, the dog died again, found in the same place in the shadows under the tree. He stayed dead, this second time, and as soon as he was gone, the daughter lost all her new words. She did not become ill again, only went back to speaking as a young girl, as she had before. It was only much later, when she learned complicated words in school, and felt their familiar shapes in her mouth, that she was reminded of her childhood illness.

A Snake's Tongue Is Forked

EVERYONE'S HEARD OF A HOOP SNAKE—it takes its tail in its mouth and rolls like a hoop, like a wheel, chasing a person or child or animal. It has a stinger on its tail, and if the snake rolls into a tree, if the stinger gets stuck in a tree, that tree will die.

She might have seen one, a hoop snake, might say she has. Tonight she's in the bedroom where no one sleeps anymore, where the furniture is gone and the window is dirty and the flowered wallpaper is cracked. What brought her here, into this room where her grandmother died, here in the night with her face pressed against the wall?

She followed a crack in the basement's cement floor where it bent and forked along the wall next to the stairs, across the door frame, across the kitchen tiles. It is a line, a map, a piece of string to follow, wound tight around the house, squeezing all the time and the people in the rooms in those times, all the conversations and misunderstandings.

A crack is a snake. A snake is a line, a forking line. Is a snake's tongue forked? A snake's tongue is forked.

The roses in the wallpaper, the carnations, the vines cut in two by the crack so they should fall but they do not fall. She leans close, her nose almost touching, her eyelashes brushing the wall. Pay attention. There are other layers, old paper, the choices of other people, the smell of old paste that would go to powder if she took hold of the crack and tore it open, spilling the snake all lengthwise.

If you sneak up behind a rattlesnake and take it by the tail, crack it like a whip, you can snap the head clean off its body. What if the head flipped back and bit you, in the hand or neck or face, if there was still venom in its fangs? There's a difference between poisonous and venomous. You should know it, should learn it. Heads without bodies are more dangerous, somehow more desperate and unpredictable, not moving in any way that is a pleasure to see, never saying anything you want to hear.

She is intent, not losing her way, following each fork, doubling back. In the window behind her, a black dog could be running up the street, a full moon hanging; a head, a human head could float past, faintly smiling behind the glass. A snake cannot move on a sheet of glass. A snake on ice is useless. Snakes are shy creatures and we are only beginning to find out more about how they live. A bird or a mammal, these are animals that can learn from experience. Snakes are deaf and have no eyelids and cannot learn like this.

Once she saw a snake's head loose in the garden, its long body divided into five pieces by the blade of a mower. Joint snakes, if you hit one it breaks up into pieces as long as your finger. A bull snake blows like a bull when it gets riled. A coachwhip snake has a braided tail. It'll wrap around a person or animal and whip with its plaited tail until that person or child or animal has run them themself to death.

She moves slowly, carefully. She is halfway through the house; she wonders if the crack is circular, if it will connect to itself like a hoop snake, or if it will never end. A snake will not stop growing because its enclosure is small. That is a myth.

She believes all sorts of things, she is willing, she will follow anything that pulls her attention. This wallpaper is flocked, in vertical strips, the white flowers pressing up through the gray, the foliage, leaves holding the cool shadows below, the space where a snake can sleep or hide or be discovered, where it might slip into the open, peek its head out from under, its red tongue keeping time.

Remember the joint snake, all broken up, left behind in the yard? If you don't bury the head, if you leave it out with the rest, it will search for the other pieces, sniffing here and there with its tongue jerking in and out. By morning that snake will be whole again.

Noon, Eye, Racecar, Kayak

THE BACK YARD HAS NO FENCE. The crabgrass gives way to the trees of the forest, out behind Naomi's grandmother's house; night begins under the trees and then creeps out into the neighborhood. Someone has drawn on these trees' trunks in white chalk, the outlines of people, so it seems a legion of ghosts stands there, arising out of the darkness as one goes deeper.

Naomi and Sonja walk away from the house. They have been drinking tea, reading a notebook of old stories, and now as they walk they're trying out the insults they found there, using them as twisted endearments.

"If you go away," Sonja says, "I'll turn your hands and feet to ice bear claws."

"I'll pull your bones out one by one."

They kiss, then walk deeper, beyond the chalk people, past the whine of the fiberglass factory on the other side of the fence. The girls stay under the trees.

They hold hands for a moment; they let each other loose. Sonja wears a dark dress, black boots, a baseball cap. Naomi, a black t-shirt, jeans, sandals. The air has a chill now, shimmering blue lights through the trees ahead.

"I'll throw my dog up in the sky and he'll defecate all over your village," Naomi says. "I'll stuff fox ghosts into the nose of your kayak and they'll chew off your feet with their sharp teeth while you paddle."

Sonja laughs. "Kayak's one of those words."

"What words?"

"Where it's spelled the same forward and backward. It's called something."

There's a sound ahead, a faint hum, the filter of the swimming pool, but there are no voices, no people, just empty chairs around the pool deck, inside the iron fence. White steam rises from the water, the lights in the pool the only lights, shining up through the steam onto the green leaves of the tall trees' branches.

"What if someone comes?" Naomi says.

Sonja pulls her dress over her head, bends down to unlace her boots. Her pale, white back glows in the moonlight, the knobs of her spine, her sharp shoulder blades as she climbs over the fence. She turns to offer Naomi a hand.

"Come on," she says. "What, are you going to wear wet underwear the rest of the night?"

"I'll figure it out."

"It's just you and me."

"I'll crack your leg bones," Naomi says. "I'll crack them to sharp splinters that will push out through your skin. How would that feel?"

The girls slip into the water at the corner of the pool, where there are steps, metal handrails. The water is cold, a line around their ankles, then warmer as they slide in. They don't jump, for they want to be silent, not to alert the people in the motel, the dark windows where people might be sleeping.

In the middle of the pool, the girls are hidden by the steam. Close together, they bump against each other, drift apart. Naomi sees Sonja's hand, flashing close, then half her face.

"Why is it so different at night? The water feels different."

"Softer and heavier, too."

"We couldn't ever get caught."

"No one would ever understand."

Naomi sinks down, into the bright blue, Sonja's long white leg. She surfaces again.

"How would it be, if I cut off your head?"

"Bloody, and it would hurt. Could you do it really fast?"

"Depends on the knife or whatever. I don't know if I could do it at all. Really I'd like nothing better than to just tear your heart out through your mouth without any cutting."

"What would it taste like?"

The girls laugh and splash, then both go under. Sonja's fingers circle Naomi's ankle; Naomi takes hold of Sonja's hip, the sharp curve of bone. They let loose, rise again.

"Let's trade names."

"Clothes, at least."

"Does it hurt to drown?"

"A little, probably. I heard freezing to death is best. You just fall asleep. Drowning is second best."

"You cough?"

"Your lungs fill up. You cough air out and breathe water in—"

"What do you see?"

"I don't know. That's really the question, you're right."

The girls sink down again. Naomi swoops low, her black hair floating around her face so she can't see, her hands flat on the smooth floor of the pool. And then Sonja grabs her from behind, above, soft breasts against Naomi's back as she tries to turn.

The girls hold each other, hands on shoulders, arms, legs kicking around. They stay under, start to rise, don't surface, and the water swirls and shifts around them, turning from its bright blue toward purple, darker and darker. Naomi coughs without surfacing, and water slips past her lips, into her mouth. It tastes dirty, like metal; she opens her eyes and there is no light. Kicking down, finding the gritty floor, she fights upwards, coughing to the surface, pulling Sonja after her.

It is so bright, it is no longer night, the sky a solid blue overhead.

The water isn't blue, it is brown, impossible to see through.

This is not the same pool at all; there are no buildings, nearby, nothing, a kind of desert. On three sides there is only sand, a line of horizon. No camels, no pyramids, though they would not look out of place. Low mountains, brown hills, mark the other side, behind the girls; closer, a pale brick wall stretches so far it seems to have no end.

This pool is tiled, different shades of pale blue, stained rusty along the water-line, rust marks on the blue tiled deck that stretches a foot or so to the dark, sharp-looking grass. There is a strip of grass, and then sand. A row of broken trees, twenty feet high with a few wispy branches on top. A kind of tree the girls have never seen, and there's no shade at all from the blazing sun, the blue sky bright in every direction.

"Naomi," Sonja says. Her voice is a whisper. "Look."

Naomi turns slowly. The water reflects the sun. She squints, and then, twenty feet away in the corner of the pool, she sees the man's head. The dark water circles his neck, so the head seems disembodied. It is perfectly still, and then the eyes blink, watching the girls. The head is completely bald; the man's face is wrinkled, with a large nose, ears that stick out along the tops.

"Where are we?" Naomi says, and with that the head begins to move, still facing them, sliding away to the far side of the pool.

"Wait," Sonja says. "Where are you going?"

"Nowhere," the man says, after a pause. "There's nowhere to go." He stops, at the wall of the pool; on the edge, there is a glass mug. Slowly, a hand surfaces. The man picks up the mug, dips it into the pool, takes a long drink of the dark water.

"I thought I broke my legs," he says, "and they healed. It's the minerals in the water that does it. I used to wear glasses, and now my eyes are fine, perfect."

Naomi watches Sonja watching the man. She can see Sonja's clavicles, straight across, an inch under the line of dark water, and her pale chest, her pale nipples, but she can see no deeper.

"Did you follow me here?" the man says. "What do you want?"

"Nothing," Naomi says.

"We didn't try," Sonja says. "Where are we?"

"In some in-between place," he says. "Does it matter?"

Naomi slides her feet along the solid, gritty bottom of the pool. There is no hole she can feel, no easy way from there to here, or from here to there. The sun shines hot atop her head, her hair already drying, the strap of her bra sharp at her shoulder.

"Please," the man says. "I never meant anything." Now he moves further away, looking out toward the mountains. "I didn't follow you here, you followed me. I'm not ready for you."

"We did not," Sonja says. "We don't know you."

"Noon, eye, racecar," he says.

"What?"

"A palindrome," he says, "is the same, backward and forward."

Naomi startles, Sonja's hand suddenly touching her shoulder.

"Where is this?" Sonja says.

"Only some words can do it," he says. "Are there other types of things that might be the same, backward and forward? Is anything really the same if you turn it around, even those words?"

"Who are you?"

"I had a name," he says. "But I don't know if I have a name, here, if there's a reason for a name in this place." He turns a slow circle, ripples swirling away from him, and then faces the girls again. "When I had a name, my name was Oscar, but I don't expect I'll be in this place much longer, or whether in the next place names will be used."

There are no clouds in the blue sky, no airplanes, no wind or sound, no roads, no birds or animals, no cars, nothing.

"Kayak," Naomi says. "A kayak is the same, if you turn it around."

"Perhaps." The man winces a kind of smile. "Depending on the shape, the stern might as well be the bow." He returns his attention to the mug, takes another long drink. "It's difficult to imagine a kayak, in this heat," he says, "to think of a girl like you traveling across the ice, the snowfields, all that weather and those animals."

"What are you talking about?"

"You don't recognize me," he says. "Why would you recognize me?"

He sets down the glass mug and then sinks lower, again, so the dark water circles his neck. Silently his head slides back and forth on the surface. Slowly, very gradually, it sinks lower. His chin is gone, his mouth, his nose. Soon only his eyes, deep in shadow, are visible, and then only the top of his head, like the shell of a white turtle, slipping and zigzagging, closer and closer.

Finally even that slips under, and the girls wait, pressed against each other. They wait a minute, then another, staring at the spot in the water where the head had last been, where the man might surface if he were not closer, reaching out beneath the dark water.

Naomi takes Sonja's left hand in her right, swings her around, close. The girls hold each other, arms wrapped around, faces so close, eyes staring into eyes. They breathe in—one long, hot breath—and then they close their eyes and go under.

Hands have brains, and hearts. Every finger does.

It's as if the pool's gritty bottom has dropped away, disappeared. The girls sink through the dark water, away from the sunlight above. Deeper and deeper they go, until it is impossible to know what is up and where is down. Their legs kick each other as they rise through the blue water, bright blue.

They break through the ceiling, gasping in the night, surrounded by steam. The stars above. The tall pine trees stretching into the sky.

And then, suddenly: footsteps, the shape of a man circling the pool, the jangle of keys. The girls are silent, they pull their heads low, invisible in the steam. There's the sound of a door opening, then a switch, and then all the lights are suddenly gone, the water black around them.

Naomi feels Sonja's fingers, gently circling her wrist. The girls wait silently, then slowly slide out toward the edge, the stairs, the steel handrails faintly glowing. They rush across the concrete pool deck, to the fence, over the fence.

The girls are safe under the trees, in the shadows. They struggle to pull their dry clothes over their wet bodies and already they're hurrying away from the pool, shoes untied. Ahead, deeper in the forest, they hear voices—do they hear voices?—and faint laughter, but they can't catch up. Then there is only silence, the faint wind in the branches above.

When the girls find themselves back amid the chalk people, surrounded by the ghosts on the trees, they cry out in relief.

The Earth Will Know

A WOMAN GAVE BIRTH to a creature of the dusk, bristle-skinned and splotchy, its face a puckered snout, its limbs all mismatched. No one could identify what it was, so the grandmother said, Bristle or no, the earth will know. They killed the creature and buried it in the snow, to learn what kind of thing it was. In time the ghost came back: a pretty little black-haired girl.

Of course as the girl grew she became devoted to her grandmother. The old woman could see things no one else could, even if some said she was out of her wits.

When the grandmother died, she sent the girl on a journey, deep into the snow country. This was the land of the ice bears with their thick white fur, their sharp claws and razor teeth, with their mighty penises dragging like tails. The bears ranged and ranged hungrily through the snowfields, but this did not stop the girl. She desired to please her grandmother.

The snow around her stifled all sound as she walked. Snow fell through the air, taking even the whisper of her breath. The sky glowed faintly, the sun impossible to locate, her shadow pale against the snow. This shadow strayed, cut loose as if looking for something, or a better person to attach itself to, then circled back, sliding along beneath her. It was her only company, and she was not far from the precipice, where a spirit collected human heads and sucked snot from their noses when it was hungry. She squinted to see where she was going. White, white, white. In her head, she repeated the words of her grandmother: Bristle or no, the earth will know. These words always calmed her, even here where an ice bear's white fur would be so difficult to see against the snowfield. Bristle or no, the earth will know.

At once the girl fell deep into a snowdrift. The more fiercely she struggled and swam, the deeper she sank. She remembered, then, being buried as a baby, and feared that if she climbed back out into the world she would again be the bristle-skinned creature with mismatched limbs. She held still in the perfect silence of the snowdrift and tried to decide what to do next.

This happened not far from the land of the dog-head people, who bark instead of speaking, who can be gentle husbands to human wives. This happened yet closer to the place where all men grow long beards to cover the scars on their throats.

When the girl climbed out of the snowdrift, she was still a girl, except her shadow was nowhere to be found. She wondered if it had gotten caught in the drift, but she did not dare to go inside the snow again. Also, she remembered the disloyal manner in which the shadow had been behaving, and suspected it might have slipped away earlier.

The sky shone only faintly darker than the snow, and on that line of horizon she saw distant shapes, large and dark. Elk or horses or cattle, or perhaps some other creature she had never seen. She walked in that direction. This girl had the power of sensing not only the weather of the sky but also the weather that people sent out from their bodies, and the weather of trees and rocks and other animals. She sensed that the large animals ahead, whatever kind they were, held pleasant weather in their awkward bodies.

Yet when she reached where they had stood, she found only deep footprints. Unable to read which way they had gone, she spread some of her scant dried meat around, in case the beasts returned and were hungry.

Now she came into a stretch of trees. Beneath them, it was easier to walk, for the snow was less deep. The branches high above held the snow and sometimes it sifted down around her. Once or twice it fell in larger amounts with a startling, hollow sound, and she turned, alarmed.

On a branch above, an owl looked down and suddenly said, "Bristle or no, the earth will know."

"Grandmother?" the girl said, but the owl only closed its yellow eyes and turned its head away.

It was then that the girl felt her shadow return, hinged back to her body. She was heartened, for this meant that the shadow had failed to find a more fortunate situation.

Embark, Depart, Discover

NAOMI EXPECTED THE SHIP TO SHIFT IN THE WATER as she stepped off the ramp that stretched away from the dock, but it did not. The ship was larger than the dock, so large that she was unable to see it all; now she was on the ship and she didn't know what it looked like.

A short, bearded man in a white uniform rushed to meet her. He pointed down a narrow deck, toward some metal stairs.

"Hello," she said.

Taking her suitcase, he led her deeper into the ship. Up more stairs, switching back, climbing, then down narrow hallways. The man turned slightly, to check that she was following. His face was serious, his black hair combed slick and shining. His body was slim, his skin dark, his fingers long and slender.

A few times Naomi glimpsed other people—other crewmembers in white uniforms, all similar to the man who carried her suitcase, who did not slow down.

Now they were inside the ship, there was no view of the water or the dock or the city beyond. Fire extinguishers on walls, thick hoses folded behind glass. Signs with lightning bolts on them indicated electricity, hidden away behind doors. Her guide, his key ring held at least twenty keys, and stretched out from his hip on a retractable chain as he opened door after door after door.

"Here." He stopped so suddenly she almost ran into him, then turned to look into her face. "Do you have hunger, Miss?"

"No."

He opened one last door, but did not go inside. "Do you require anything?"

"I don't think so." She saw then that there was a blue slip of paper with the letter N written on it, taped to the center of the door.

"In that case," he said, "I'll be back in a short time."

With that, he disappeared down the hallway.

Naomi stepped into her cabin. It was white, everything so white and clean—the cabinet, the walls, the metal shelves, the blanket on the single bed. The chair was white, and the small table. She pulled a white curtain aside, revealing a white toilet, and a small shower, a white towel hanging neatly from a hook.

Turning, she looked at her blue suitcase, in the middle of the room; it seemed too ragged, too bright. Should she unpack, put her things away? She had no idea how long a journey this would be. Somewhere in the suitcase was a copy of her grandmother's will, but she didn't need to read it; she'd memorized the section that forecast where she was right now:

I bequeath to my granddaughter Naomi a journey by sea. A voyage, and more than a voyage. The details of this journey have been arranged, and shall remain secret. If she chooses to embark, she will discover the secrets, and she will find the person who requires her assistance. Whether or not she accepts her journey is her choice, but one she must make within one year of my passing.

Naomi stood still for a moment, in the middle of her white cabin. She had embarked on her journey. To embark was to step onto a bark, which was another name for a boat. She didn't know if that was how it worked. She wondered if to depart meant to come apart, if discover meant the same as uncover.

Her cabin had one small window. Square, not round like the port-hole she'd imagined. Stepping close to it, she could see the dock, far below; after a moment, she recognized the tiny shapes of her parents, of her younger brother, Justin. They turned and walked away, toward where their blue car was parked. Her father hadn't wanted her to go, had always mistrusted what he called his mother-in-law's "mysteries." Naomi's mother had only said that Naomi was an adult, at least legally, and would have to make up her own mind. Neither of them seemed aware that this journey was a way to satisfy a dead person's final wish, a chance to be surprised.

Further up the dock, Naomi saw her friends, Sonja and Alex. She recognized them by Alex's orange stocking cap, which he wore even though the day was warm and sunny.

Naomi took her phone from her pocket, dialed; Sonja was far below, tiny, but it was still possible to see her take out her own phone, holding it up to see who was calling.

"Hi."

"Hello."

"I miss you already," Sonja said.

"You said that last night. I can see you."

"You can?"

"Look up. I'm standing in the window."

Sonja looked up, her pale face flashing, shielding her eyes with her free hand. "There's a million windows," she said, "and the sun's reflecting in them."

Naomi tried to open the window, so she could stick out her head or wave an arm, but the window didn't open.

"You're moving," Sonja said. "The boat's moving. Are you nervous?"

"I can't feel it," Naomi said, though now she saw that there was a gap, dark water widening between the ship and dock. "It's weird," she said, "I had this idea of the boat as having sails, like some sort of pirate ship, with masts and spars, one of those crow's nests."

"Smokestacks," Sonja said. "That's what it has."

Naomi could still see Sonja by pressing her face against the cool window, looking back. "What does it look like?" she said. "Now I'm on it and I have no idea how to imagine myself where I am. We drove up and we were already so close to it."

"It's like a building," Sonja said. "Or a couple of buildings, floating away. It's got all these big metal boxes—orange and yellow and blue— stacked on top of each other everywhere. They were doing that with a crane."

"And people?"

"Only the men working on it, but they wear those white uniforms, and the boat is white, so that makes them really hard to see. Especially now, when you're farther away."

There was a pause, static, wind and water.

"Have they told you where you're going?" Sonja said.

"No."

"Or when you'll come back?"

"Nothing," Naomi said. "Not yet."

"I miss you."

"My room looks like a hospital room, only smaller."

"Alex says he misses you, too, but I miss you more."

"Is there a name on the back of the ship?" Naomi said.

"What? No, not that I can see."

"Did anyone say a name?"

"Of the boat?" Sonja said. "No. I wish I was coming with you."

Naomi could feel the rumble of the ship's engines in the floor, through her shoes, the soles of her feet, but she did not feel movement, the sense of flotation, of shifting water. Then there was a click, and the phone felt different against her ear.

"Hello?" she said, but there was no answer. She could no longer see Sonja, or the dock; she could see the shore, the land, but suddenly she had no reception. She tried again, then stepped back from the window and put the phone in her pocket.

Lifting the suitcase up onto the bed, she unzipped but didn't open it. Instead, she crossed the cabin in two steps, opened the door, and stepped into the hallway. She half-expected an alarm, or at least a person to be there, to direct her, but there was no one, no sound except her breathing, her footsteps.

It was a short hallway, perhaps twenty feet long, with a door on either end. The door to her room, the N taped to it, and three other doors along the passageway. All locked, all marked with the lightning bolt. Naomi walked to one end of the hall—the door the man had brought her through, she believed. This one was also locked. Turning, she passed a fire extinguisher, the flat coils of a fire hose. Also an ax, with a red metal head and a silver blade, sharp behind its glass. A small hammer hung next to the glass, to break it, in case of emergency.

She tried her phone again—nothing—as she passed her cabin, then turned the handle on the door at the other end of the hallway. This one opened.

Immediately the air smelled salty, fishy, and like diesel; the ship's engines were louder, humming and hovering as she stepped out onto the deck, into the wind.

The dark is another kind of ocean.

It was an observation deck, it seemed, about twenty feet square with a few rows of yellow benches, bolted down. She stepped to the white railing and looked across the flat, blue water. It was far below, stretching to the coast, which was at least a mile away, low mountains and pale buildings. She leaned out and looked down along the side of the boat. She walked the perimeter, along the railing. Now she saw the metal storage containers, stacked three high or more, far below on the wide, lower decks. White lifeboats hung along the edge of the ship, suspended by chains. She could see into them, piles of orange life preservers. She could not see any people below, no movement at all.

Overhead, two smokestacks coughed black clouds into the sky. Next to them, a white arm, probably radar, circled and searched. There were no flags anywhere, no seagulls. The sky was so much paler than the ocean.

Naomi sat down on the hard yellow bench. She bent her head forward, then rolled it from one side to the other, letting the swirling wind lift her hair, blow it all around her. Then, beyond the hum of the engines, through it, she heard a smaller sound—a clicking—and she swept her hair out of her eyes just in time to see a man's head, leaning out from the deck above, a camera in front of his face.

"Hey!" she said, standing. "What are you doing?"

"Taking your photograph," he said.

She squinted upward; twenty feet away, he appeared to be the same man who led her to her cabin, but she couldn't be certain.

"Fine," she said, "but I don't see why you have to be so sneaky about it."

With that, he pulled his head back, and she couldn't see him any longer.

She sat down again and looked across at the mountains. Smaller boats passed, heading in the opposite direction, toward the harbor. She was about to go back inside, to unpack her suitcase, when the door opened and the man appeared, smiling, still holding the camera.

"So it is in fact quite fine with you?" he said. "For me to take your photograph?"

"Who are you?" she said.

"I am Joachim, of course. And you, you are Naomi. I know that."
He lifted the camera, squinted through it. "Now, that's right, that's
perfect. Don't smile too much."

When he was finished, he put a lens cap on the camera and let it hang
around his neck. His beard and hair were the exact same length, connected like a helmet, with a chin strap, an oval around his mouth, his
lips, his white teeth as he smiled at her. His dark eyes were set wide;
his small ears stuck out. There were two gold rings in his ears, a thin
gold chain around his neck.

"And how is your journey, thus far, Naomi? Your cabin? Do you
have hunger?"

"Where are the other passengers?" she said.

"Who?"

"Are there other passengers on this ship?"

"This ship is not a passenger ship, Miss."

"So what am I?"

"A passenger," he said, and smiled. "Yes, it is a paradox. A passenger on
a ship that is not a passenger ship! A kind of riddle?"

"Yes," she said.

"I've been assured that everything is prepared for you," he said. "And if
there are things that you need or desire, you may request them of me.
I am your liaison."

"But you don't know why."

"I was chosen because I am the one who has the most of your language."

"This is your job?" she said. "Looking after me?"

"Certainly not!" He reached out a hand, and she thought he might
touch her, but he merely rested it on the yellow bench in front of
the one she was sitting on. "In fact, I work in the kitchen, helping
the cook to prepare the meals. That is my occupation. Acting as your
liaison is an additional responsibility, and also an honor."

Joachim sat down next to her on the bench, their thighs almost touching, and then he suddenly stood up and moved to the bench in front and spun to face her. It seemed he had something to say, but he only smiled.

"Will we follow the coast," she said, "all the way to where we're going?"

He frowned. "Where we're going? I can't say that we're going anyplace together, Miss."

"The ship, I mean."

"Possibly we are going the same place," he said. "Perhaps we are."

"You don't know?"

"I'll always be on the boat," he said. "I do not know what is true, for you. With you, I'm told there are secrets."

"You don't know?"

"Correct. Not with any certainty. I am here to help you."

"Can I walk around the rest of the ship? The doors are locked."

"That is for your safety," he said. "It's a very dangerous ship, it can be."

"Maybe you could show me around?"

Joachim stood, straightened the seams of his white slacks.

"We will not follow the coast," he said, "for that is not typically the way we proceed. If we do follow the coast, that would be unusual and surprising, but it would not be mistaken, should that be our course." He checked behind him, looking to the deck above, then to the door that led to the hallway. "I must now go," he said. "You and I will surely talk more. And before long I shall return with your meal, so you might settle yourself in any intervening time."

"Thank you," she said.

The camera bounced on his chest, all the keys jangled on their ring at his hip. He went through the white door and was gone.

Hello

WHEN YOU SEE ME, then you'll know things are about to become interesting! I am lighthearted, but I don't fool around. Sometimes I greet a visitor by saying, "Hello, I'm dreaming," which is a compliment and then, at the same time, a kind of fact.

I can become, like anyone, overcome by tenderness.

Help me. Don't be afraid. My eyes were so hazy and then they got better and then turned worse again. I live in hope as I wander in shadows.

I wear eyeglasses. I wear a white undershirt for four days before I wash it. I wear the shirt frontward, backward, then inside-out in both directions. On the fourth day you can see the tag, here, beneath my beard, like a little white tongue with writing on it. M. I am a medium-sized man, requesting your assistance.

If I were to tell you that I'm a dead man with this long gray beard, walking around on these bandy-assed legs, would that change anything?

An old person telling a story of when they were young—even when it's interesting, it can be very difficult to believe. Or, more plainly: such stories are unbelievable. To the listener, to the teller. There are stories in my mind that I suspect arrive from somewhere else, not my past.

Does it matter? Listen. I have images in my mind I don't recognize, I see people in my photographs who might be me. Can I attach myself to a story, project myself into a picture? Is there a difference, if I believe it?

I believe everything. I am certain of nothing. I'll be delighted to see you coming.

Hello, I'm dreaming. Take for instance this photograph, here: a man wearing nothing but boots, backward on a spotted horse, lying flat, his dark mustache near the horse's tail. Are they moving? There's snow everywhere, a thicket of trees. That man might be me. Am I being punished, or am I playing around? I've always been lighthearted, I've always delighted in the weather. I like to think of myself, this adventurer. I'm the kind of person who wouldn't ask for help until the last moment. Listen to me.

I'm somewhere between a person like you and the dead person I said I was. Or I am dead, and still talking, unbelievable. It frustrates me when you anxious people insist that a story or dream, a ghost or memory must arise from, must be grounded in a person, a place, a time. Do you honestly believe one must come before the other? Look at me. Things like that can't flow in any one direction.

A Conversation at Sea

"THERE'S BLUE IN EVERY DIRECTION," she said. "All this water. How far is it to land?"

"Quite some distance, I should think," he said. "At night, the water is black."

"Are we closer to where we're going?"

"We must be, Miss, but it's only the second day of your journey."

"Which will take how long?"

"I know as much as you do, Miss. I can only see to your requirements. I brought some books from the library and left them in your cabin."

"You went into my room?"

"I certainly did. You'll find the books on the small table adjacent to your bed."

"The water is the same color at night," she said. "It's only that we can't see it."

"That is not in fact the truth," he said, "but I have no desire to argue with you, and indeed I am not allowed disputes of that nature with you.

"Will you be needing anything else?"

"What are the sounds I heard last night? The knocking, and the shouting, and the music?"

"Did it unnerve you, Miss?"

"It kept me awake," she said. "But not for too long."

"I will note this," he said. "And I can inform you that what you are hearing are games of ping-pong. Do you know this sport? The excellent paddles? The crew's recreation room is on the floor beneath your cabin. We also perform karaoke. This is the singing with pre-recorded music."

"And where is the library?" she said. "Could you take me there?"

"There are rules onboard a ship," he said. "A ship can be a dangerous place, and the rules help keep us safe."

"Is the library a dangerous place?"

"As you know, Miss, it has been decided that you must be restricted to your cabin and this observation deck. This ship is not a passenger ship, and so we are not prepared for passengers. This is why I am here, why it has become my responsibility to satisfy your requirements and to answer your questions."

"How many people are on the boat?"

"On this ship? Several hundred, I should think. The crew, and then the captain and officers, who are in another part of the ship."

"Can you take me there?"

"Certainly not, Miss! Not even I can enter those areas of the ship."

"So you don't talk to the captain?"

"What would I say to the captain? I have never even seen the captain, and I believe that if I were to meet him, we could not converse."

"Have you seen a picture of him?"

"The captain will speak Dutch, Miss. Or he will speak German. These are the languages the officers are said to speak, and they are not languages I possess."

"But you're the only one who speaks English?"

"I have the most English, yes. That is what I've been told, and why I am here, serving you, Miss. It's possible that the officers or even the captain might speak English, but that is not a fact that I can verify."

"So what language does the crew speak?"

"Primarily Tagalog, for they hail largely from the Philippines."

"And that's where you're from?"

"I do speak Tagalog," he said, "but I did not state that that's where I'm from. I live now on this ship."

"Does it have a name?"

"This ship? It does not."

"I thought all ships had names."

"Perhaps," he said, "but that name has not been made known to me. It is difficult to see, if it is written on the stern, when one is on the boat."

"Yes," she said. "Exactly."

"Is there more that I can do for you, this afternoon, Miss? Other questions?"

"How deep do you think the ocean is, here?"

"I should think that it is quite, quite deep."

Shadows and Skeletons

THE FOREST PRESSES IN, close against the houses in the neighborhood. It is night, late at night, most of the windows dark. One window, on a second floor, is alight. In that room, in that bedroom, are Alex and Sonja.

"What's so funny?" she says.

"This notebook," he says. "Did the old lady make all this up?"

"I don't know where she got it."

This house belongs to their friend Naomi's grandmother. When Naomi went away, she asked Alex to watch over things. Tonight he sits on a bed, pushed against the wall, beneath a window. A mirror has been dragged off to one side, next to the closet. Sonja sits on a folding chair, a tall glass of water on the wooden floor near her bare feet. She has been here for almost an hour. Alex hadn't been expecting her. She came down the driveway, called through the kitchen window.

"It's a conversation," he says now, reading, "between a dead man and his wife:

"'It was very unkind of you to kill me.'

"'But you were already dead.'

"'To kill a person who is already dead,' he says, 'That is the unkindest thing of all.'"

Sonja drinks from her glass of water. "I always remember the time Naomi's grandma read my tea leaves." She peers into her glass, speaks in an old lady's voice: "You'll be a very good friend—"

"And she died in this room?"

"Right in that bed," Sonja says. "That's what Naomi told me. Her grandma was reading that notebook and drinking orange juice."

Alex stands up. He closes the notebook and drops it.

"I've been sleeping in that bed. You should have told me."

Sonja stretches, reaching to pick up the notebook. The notebook is blue, the pages covered in the old woman's tiny handwriting, all in sharp pencil. The writing tells of whales and ghosts, ice bears that change shape.

"'You are only skeletons,'" Sonja reads. "'Stop behaving as if you were human beings.'" She closes the notebook and sets it on the floor.

The room is silent. Overhead, the square glass lampshade cradles dead flies. Cracks fork across the flowered wallpaper.

"You miss her," Alex says. "Naomi."

"Yes."

"Did you want to see me, tonight, or did you come because of her?"

"Because of Naomi?"

"I mean, because this place reminds you of her, of being here with her."

"I don't know. Both, I guess. It does remind me of her, and I wanted to see you. And I wasn't doing anything." Sonja looks across at him, smiles. "I kind of think Naomi asked you to stay here to bring me and you together."

Are fireflies dangerous to girls?

Standing, she crosses the room and turns off the light, the switch next to the hallway. Then she goes to each window and adjusts the shades. Light shines in one window, from the streetlamp: a pale yellow band two feet high, cast across the room, onto the opposite wall. She stands in that light and the shape of her body, a shadow with her head cut off, settles black against the wall.

"What are you doing?" Alex says.

Sonja is already on the floor, her hands up in the light. On the wall, the shadows change shape, slide along. A dog's head, a face, a swooping bird whose wings are her fingers. A duck, or goose, a boy's face, an elephant with a dangling trunk. A boat. A rabbit, a flower, two bears.

"You have skills," Alex says.

"Here," she says. "Stand up. Put your hand on my hip, then step back. Keep moving. Slow."

Sonja is closer to the window, her shadow so much bigger; Alex's hands, stretched toward the light, are huge. He steps closer to the door and his shadow bends, winnows to a strip and then disappears into the darkness of the hallway. He steps back and his shadow returns, pulling itself loose from the larger shadow like a body from dark water.

Sonja reaches out, her hand on the cool skin of his neck, then lets loose again, drifts to the other side of the room.

"You're taking off your shirt?" he says.

"Does that bother you?"

"No."

"It does, doesn't it?"

In the dim light, Alex can see her smile.

"Look at me," she says. "No, my shadow, I mean—otherwise the shadow just looks like a blob, you see? Look at you, how your shirt is."

Alex pulls his shirt over his head, stands next to her.

"It'd be better if we were skeletons," he says, "the shadows, then."

"We're human beings," she says. "Behaving like human beings."

The only wind in the room is from their bodies, moving around each other in the darkness, in and out of the light, the cool air on their bare skin. The ceiling creaks, a cracking sound.

"What's that?" Sonja says.

"The house." Alex looks up at the ceiling, the cracks in the plaster.

And then a scratch of branches across the shingles.

"Only the trees," he says.

A knock above, on the rooftop. Another.

"I want to see." Sonja picks up her shirt and goes out the door, into the hallway. Alex hurries after her, clattering down the stairs, through the kitchen.

In the back yard, the grass is cold against their feet. Sonja stands buttoning her shirt; Alex looks past her, points into the forest.

Against the black shadows, the white outlines of people glow. The white shapes—some legless, some with their arms stretched over their heads—mark the dark tree trunks here and there, more figures further away, deeper in the shadows.

"I know," Sonja says. "Naomi and I saw them, before. It's chalk."

One pine tree leans close against the house, its branches stretching over the top so it would be easy to climb up, to peek in the windows, to keep going and then drop down onto the roof. Sonja starts to reach for a low branch, then follows Alex as he goes around the side of the house, out toward the street. Barefoot, still, they walk out onto the blacktop, its surface warm from the day. They walk back far enough from the house that they can see the bare rooftop.

"No one up there," Sonja says.

"I like being with you," he says.

"I know," she says. "Me, too. Look—"

In the upstairs window, then, in the yellow strip of light, they see two shadows. The shadows are the shapes of two people, human bodies slipping through the light, overlapping, coming apart, standing still for a moment. Two outstretched hands reaching for each other and connecting, one long arm. And then the hands slip away, into the other shadows, the yellow strip of light empty again.

"Is that from before?" Alex says. "No. That can't be—"

He follows Sonja inside, breathlessly through the dining room, and up the stairs, slapping the bedroom door open.

There is no one in the room. Only the folding chair, the notebook, the glass of water on the floor.

They walk through the whole house and every room is empty.

"No one's here," Alex says. "Only the two of us, I mean."

"And shadows. This house, sometimes." Sonja shivers, hugs herself. "Let's go—"

"Where?"

"I want to swim." She takes his hand. "Let's sneak into the motel pool."

Outside again, they follow the people on the tree trunks, deeper and deeper into the forest. The white figures fade, the deeper they go: legs rubbed away, hands missing, heads gone blurry. It's as if whoever drew them had run out of chalk.

Bears

NAOMI JUMPED ROPE on the observation deck of the ship. She felt a prickling on the back of her neck, her shoulders, someone watching her, and she spun a slow circle—hopping, the rope whooshing overhead, snapping against the deck, beneath her feet—but saw no one on the higher sections of the ship, above and behind her. The other three directions: dark blue ocean, no land in sight. Below, past the suspended lifeboats, orange, blue and yellow storage containers were stacked high across the wide lower decks.

She tried to cross her arms in front of her body, and the rope snarled and twisted, almost tripping her. She began again, the rope sweeping through the sky, cutting the horizon, into the ocean, around and around. The words of her grandmother's will circled, too: The details of this journey have been arranged, and shall remain secret. If she chooses to embark on this journey, she will discover the secrets, and she will find the person who requires her assistance. Naomi imagined her grandmother, watching her, now, and wondered what was planned, and how much could be certain. She wondered if a secret waited without changing, or might be shifted somehow by the person who discovered it.

"Good afternoon, Miss," Joachim said, suddenly behind her, standing just out of range of the circling rope. "I see that you are exercising."

"Clearly," she said, not stopping.

"It is a good day?" he said.

"Do you watch me?" she said. "Do you spy on me?"

"Certainly!" he said. "Sometimes I do."

"Do you like it?"

"It is not a question of liking or disliking, Miss. I do it to keep you safe."

Naomi stopped jumping; she coiled the rope in her hands. "I could tie this to the railing and climb down," she said. "It would be easy for me to do."

Joachim smiled. The light caught on his gold earrings, which flashed as he rubbed his beard, then the top of his head.

"You think I couldn't?" she said. "I could also take the ax from the hallway, next to the fire hose, and chop down the door."

"Miss," he said, "you certainly could. Yet you would still be on the ship, and we'd bring you back, and you could climb down again, and we would bring you back. Now what would be the point of that? It could become humorous. If you were to damage the door with the ax, someone would fix it, and the ax might be taken away. In that case, what if there were a fire? Miss, there's nothing for you to discover on the ship, only possible dangers." He paused, clasped his long, thin fingers. "I am very pleased to see you today. And it gives me pleasure to see you using the jump rope I provided, as well."

"It's colder today," she said. "Is it getting colder?"

"It appears to be so," he said.

"What if my whole journey is on this ship?" she said. "What if I never get off, if I never go back home?"

"That would be a disappointment, Miss. Allow me to say that I believe such a journey seems unlikely. It might hardly be termed a journey at all. That might properly be termed a voyage."

"But you don't know?"

"We only know these things as they happen," he said. "And in the meantime I will keep you safe and see to your requirements."

"Is there someone in my cabin, now?"

"Certainly not! I am the only one allowed to enter your cabin. And yourself, of course. It is your cabin."

Joachim looked past Naomi, behind her, then—as if receiving a signal from someone perched elsewhere on the ship—but when she turned she couldn't see anyone. She sat down on one of the yellow benches. The sky was so pale, and the whole ship was white, and all the men wore white uniforms and were impossible to see.

"There aren't any seagulls," she said. "I thought I'd see dolphins or porpoises or something, but it's all this blue."

"Correct," he said.

"So you go into my cabin when I'm not there?"

"Miss! Of course, to gather your laundry and see to the housekeeping. I am certainly not allowed to enter your cabin when it is inhabited."

"Certainly not!" she said.

"Are you joking at me?" he said.

"With you," she said.

"No," he said. "I am not allowed to be in your cabin with you. That is clear."

"What's in all those containers?" she said, pointing below.

Joachim walked to the railing. Shielding his eyes, he whistled as if he had just noticed the containers, as if he hadn't been aware of their presence.

"This is not a passenger ship," she said. "You keep telling me that. So it's shipping things, right? Those containers could fit cars, they could fit anything."

"Automobiles," he said. "Yes, that's possible. Or perhaps other machines. Or it might not only be large items! It could be many smaller items, Miss. Hundreds or even thousands of shoes, which come in pairs. Or dominoes. Or magnifying glasses—"

"Stop," she said.

"It would make no difference." Joachim stepped close and sat next to her, close enough that his pressed white slacks touched her dirty jeans. Her hands looked so pale next to his. She twisted her hair back so it didn't blow into his face.

BEARS

"I have a question for you," he said. "It is not a question you must answer, if it causes discomfort."

"Fine," she said.

"Have you ever traveled on an airplane?" he said.

"Yes," she said. "Many times."

"Even at night?"

"Certainly," she said.

"Some nights." His voice was suddenly softer, almost a whisper. "Some black nights I can't even tell what is water and what is sky and what is land, if we are close to shore. I see fires out in the blackness and I wonder if those are places where people are together. Perhaps those fires are their emotions, or it is a place where people are disagreeing or excited by one another, that I am seeing an inside or a way between people."

As he spoke, Naomi watched the ocean, the long smooth swells that rolled on forever, searching for land, that hid so many things inside their thickness.

"Is that possible?" Joachim said. "Do you think I am only being hopeful when I speak of these fires?"

"I don't know," she said. "Maybe you're seeing campfires, and people are gathered around them, but you can't see the people?"

Joachim set his hand on her thigh for a moment, then lifted it again. "Are you sad?" he said. "You're missing something." He stood, his keys jangling from the ring at his waist. "What can I bring you?"

"You can't," she said.

"I can try."

"I miss people," she said. "My friends, who I left behind. And my grandmother, who sent me on this journey, who brought me here. She's dead, now."

"I'm very sorry," Joachim said. "I am sorry to hear of your loss."

"I thought you might know that, somehow."

"I did not. My condolences, Miss."

A horn blew, somewhere, and then there was silence again, or actually the usual, constant hum of the engines. Above, the smokestacks leaked clouds the same color as the sky. The white radar arm spun and spun.

"You must have friends," she said. "Here on the ship."

Joachim sat down again, this time on the bench in front of her. It was awkward, the way the benches were bolted down, all facing the same way. She could only see one side of his face.

"Sometimes at night," he said, "when the ship is asleep, I go down to the lowest deck, closest to the water."

"Where I got on," she said. "That first day."

"I lower myself down," he said. "There are ropes, rope ladders, and I lower myself down quite close to the water. I see things. Faces, looking up at me. White faces, flashing, staring out at me, then folding away again inside the black waves."

"People's faces?" she said. "Are you crying?"

"I have to tell you, Miss, and I tell you with confidence."

"In confidence."

"I am not allowed to dispute with you." He paused for a moment, then continued: "These faces, they are silent. And the faces are not all that I see. In the black water, I see bears. They glow, they swim far below the surface."

"Bears?"

"I have a mask, a scuba mask with a round glass window that I can see through. I lean over the water and look into it and I see bodies, bodies without heads, white against the black. Floating, not swimming. Sometimes I wonder if they're in the sky, if the sky is thicker on those nights and I'm mistaken. To myself I call them bears when in fact they are not bears." Joachim gasped, a choking laugh. "It frightens me less, Miss, to think of them as bears. But this is too much, this is all I know, I should never waste your attention with a personal story. That is not encouraged and I am not certain if it is even allowed."

"Are you all right?" she said.

Joachim was standing again. Taking a crisp white handkerchief from his pocket, he wiped at his eyes, blew his nose.

People who go missing and are considered dead often turn up alive in other places, much later. People who are lost at sea can emerge from another body of water.

"I am speaking of my bears," he said, at last, "when you miss your friends. Unacceptable. Now your friend—is there one in particular? What do you miss about this particular person?"

"I just miss her, the way she is," Naomi said. "Being with her. We hold hands; I miss how she's not embarrassed of that. Once she told me about her dog that died, how she believed it would come back to life if they figured out how to bury it."

"Dogs may be resurrected," he said. "I've heard the tales."

"It's just something she believed, when she was a little girl."

"I see," he said. "And what is her name?"

"Sonja," she said.

"Sonja," he said.

"She came the day I got onboard. Maybe you saw her."

"I must go," Joachim suddenly said. "It is something that I have forgotten. A responsibility. Something that may have been misplaced."

Later, Naomi lay in bed, reading. She read one chapter of *Watership Down*, then one of *Kidnapped*. These were the books Joachim had given her, and somehow they worked together, tangling and running into each other in her mind. The talking rabbits, Fiver and Thumper, the loss of control over where or how you were going, with whom, the tunnels underground, the contrary winds, the burning documents.

Climbing out of bed, she pressed her ear to the bare floor. Silence. Not the tick-tock of the ping-pong ball, or the men's shouts, not the men's singing, no music. In that silence she tried to listen further, deeper, through the many floors, through the hull of the ship and into the night ocean, where the water became a different substance, black and silent and slippery, where the bears were swimming, floating with no heads.

What she heard was a scratching, a sandpaper sound. Her eyes opened. An envelope, sliding under the door, so close to her face. She snatched it up, she stood, she opened the door. Too slow, the hallway empty. On the envelope, her name. Written in Sonja's handwriting. The seal was already broken.

Inside an Envelope, Its Seal
Already Broken

YOU'RE NOT EVEN GONE AND ALREADY I MISS YOU. You're asleep, right next to me in bed, and I can't sleep. I could wake you, or I could talk to you in the morning, I will talk to you in the morning but I will say different things. What should I write to you? That I already miss you, that I still want to be talking to you while you're on the boat, on the ocean, moving away from me so far that you couldn't hear me if I shouted but maybe you'll have this letter which is like me talking to you. You're amazing when you sleep, with your lips barely open and the softest whistling between your teeth. I just lifted your hair out of your face so I could look at those thin pink veins in your eyelids and your lashes folded down. They're so straight and black! I have been trying to imagine how it will be with you gone, and it's hard. Especially since I don't know when you'll come back, and how different things will be, then. I suppose we'll find out. Maybe we'll do new things, but I hope we don't forget the old things. Remember when we filled the bathtub with flower petals? When we went swimming at night, sneaking into the pool? When we hid in your brother's closet and listened to him talking to himself, all about elephants and snakes and bears? I just ran my hand down your bare arm and you smiled. If you wake up, will I let you read this? I want you to sleep, I want this to be a letter. That way I can travel with you. Maybe you'll travel with me, too. I don't know if you can send me letters, but I'll think of you and I'll do the same things or things you would do. This house where you're sleeping, where I'm writing, here in your grandmother's bed, I've always been a little afraid of it, had a strange feeling even though I liked her when she was alive. If you're here with me it's all right but once you're gone, once Alex is staying here, will I come here, and what will happen? I know and you know how Alex feels about me. Once you said that you'd sleep with him, if you were me, if that's what he wanted and what would make him happy. I couldn't tell if that was just a way to say that you wanted to sleep with him. And right then I didn't want to know the answer so I didn't ask you. Now I wonder if that would remind me or make me feel like you, if I did that, what he wants to do, what you said you would do, if you were me. Maybe right now you're having a dream. In the morning I'll ask if you dreamed about me. I've never dreamed of you. I hope I do, while you're gone. I'll write it down, I'll try to send it to you, if I know where to send a letter. Outside the night is not so dark and soon it will be morning. What is it all about, the way we feel? I guess I don't really want to know. I only don't want it to stop. I only want it to slow down enough, sometimes, that I can ask the question.

Spiral Staircases

NAOMI AWAKENED TO A KNOCKING, SOMEONE AT THE DOOR. Where was she? On the ship, in her cabin. She switched on the lamp next to her bed and shadows shot away, gathering against the walls, in the corners. She rubbed her eyes.

"Miss?"

The knocking again, a pounding at the door.

She stood. Out the window, a starless sky, black, the same color as the ocean.

"Miss? It is urgent."

Naomi opened the door. Joachim stood there, smiling in the hall. She had never spoken to any other member of the crew.

"Please dress," he said, looking away. "You must come with me. I'll wait here."

"Where are we going?"

"That will soon be clear."

"What should I bring?"

"Dress, miss. That is all that is required." He pulled the door closed.

She was wearing a t-shirt, and leggings; as she pulled on a sweater, socks and shoes, he spoke to her through the door.

"Did you receive the letter from your friend?"

"Yes," she said. "I started writing back, but I didn't finish it—"

"I'll do my best to locate and send it," Joachim said. "To deliver it, to have it delivered. I will do my best, Miss."

When she opened the door, she noticed that the Joachim's white shirt was misbuttoned. His shoes were unlaced, and he appeared to be wearing only one sock.

"Are you all right?" she said. "What time is it?"

"It's time," he said, unlocking the door at the end of the hallway.

Lights switched on ahead of them, shadows racing away.

"What's happened?" she said.

"This is certainly part of the plan, Miss," he said. "Everything is in perfect order. Here, this way. Mind your step."

They went down a flight of stairs, through another doorway, outside, the floor underfoot changing to metal, to mesh. She shivered in the sharp, salty wind, smelled the diesel. They were closer to the water, now; twenty feet below, still black, yet with sudden glimpses of white foam, circling waves.

She followed Joachim down a spiral staircase, cold metal, tight, descending even closer to the surface of the ocean.

"Stay here," he said. "I shall return in a moment."

Standing in the cold, she could hear voices. Joachim's, and a deeper voice, both muffled. The sky above the ocean was growing lighter, a thick gray fog. Overhead, a white lifeboat hung like a sideways moon; with a faint ratcheting sound, it began to descend.

"Here!" Joachim said.

At first, when she turned she did not recognize him. He wore a white snowsuit, its hood pulled up, and thick rubber boots. He held out a yellow parka, black snow pants. A pair of snowmobile boots stood next to him, waiting.

"What?" she said.

"Quickly," he said. "I am told that we're racing a tide."

He helped Naomi into the yellow parka. She leaned against him as he pulled the pants over her leggings, as she stepped out of her shoes and into the boots. He offered his hand, steadied her. The boat swung slightly, still suspended, as she climbed into it.

"When are we coming back?" she said.

"Here," he said. "Mittens!"

With that, he climbed into the boat, began checking the oars. He tightened the strap of her lifejacket and then put one on himself.

"But you're supposed to tell me what's happening." She was almost shouting, now. "You're my liaison, you said."

"I have served in that capacity, yes. But I cannot tell you what I do not myself know." Joachim looked up into the sky and nodded; in a moment the boat began to descend again, bumping gently against he dark, vast side of the ship.

Naomi looked up but she could see nothing, no one. Then there was a jolt, a settling. The chains went slack. Cold spray stung her cheek. Salt. The little boat rose and fell. She had been asleep less than half an hour ago and only now, as she watched Joachim detach the chains and fit the oars in their locks, did she understand that her moment to resist, if she'd wished to resist, had slipped away.

Joachim rowed, his back to the bow, and Naomi sat in the stern, facing him. He was only five feet away, but she couldn't see his expression. The darkness, the hood pulled up with its fur ruff, his black beard jutting out. She pulled up her own hood. She fit the wool mittens over her hands. Turning, she looked back toward the ship and the ship had disappeared, swallowed by the fog. She couldn't even hear its engines; only the wind, the slap of the waves.

"Now you see," Joachim said. He shouted, his words clearer when he leaned forward, more faint as he leaned back, pulling on the oars. "You had concern about never leaving the ship, and now we have left the ship!"

"Where are we?" she said. "Where are we going?"

There were brighter spots in the fog, whorls of gray, blacker sections. And then snowflakes began drifting down. Joachim checked over his shoulder, then returned to his rowing. The waves grew louder. Now it wasn't only the slapping against the sides of the boat, the cutting of the oars, but a crashing, a breaking. A shore, somewhere ahead.

A light, an orange light, a fire in the sky. Winking, gone, there again.

"Is that one of the fires you told me about?" she said. "The ones you see at night?"

"No, Miss. That is a lighthouse."

Closer, the frosty rocks of the shoreline rose up. The squat tower of the lighthouse blended into the snow and fog. Buildings clustered next to it, on a narrow spit of rock. Joachim was rowing harder, now, checking more frequently over his shoulder. She saw that he was aiming them toward a narrow harbor, the black finger of a dock.

"Miss," he said, once they'd reached it. He stowed the oars. "Here. Provisions." He held out a small pack, helped her fit her arms through the straps. Then he took her hand, guided it to a metal ladder that was attached to the dock. Icicles hung from its rungs.

"You're not coming?" she said, but she didn't expect an answer. She took hold of the ladder, his hand on her back, steadying her, his face so close.

"I hope all goes well on the remainder of your journey," he said. "It's been my pleasure, serving you."

She climbed to the dock, then across its icy, barnacled surface. She looked down only once, at Joachim slowly turning the boat; one oar stretched back, the other forward, spindly black arms pulling against the water.

Climbing onto the stones, the land, Naomi crossed toward the lighthouse. Two telephone poles stood like bare trees, no lines on them at all, a third cracked and toppled. She stepped over it, past a white shed with its roof crushed in.

The wind cut this way, then that. Lines of frost twisted, white snakes across the rocks and between them.

She stepped onto the porch of the house. The door was open, a snowdrift in the entryway. All the windows had been blown out. A chandelier like more ice. Snow deep on the floor, the chairs, blanketing the couch. She walked through, looking for clues, but everything was blank, white. Through the kitchen, the oven's door open like a frosty tongue, and then she climbed through a window, outside. So close to the lighthouse with its orange lamp burning overhead.

The metal door was heavy, stuck. She kicked a shovel loose from the frozen ground, used its handle to wedge the door open. Inside, the whistle of wind and nothing but stairs, a spiral staircase. She climbed.

Dirt, dust and snow sifted down as she pushed the trap door open. She closed her eyes, opened them. The round room was tight and close, much quieter, its windows thick. The lamp buzzed, too bright to look at, up close, with a curved mirror behind it. Wires snaked from it to a square battery, a car battery on the floor.

Looking out, Naomi saw the triangle of Joachim's boat, barely darker than the water beneath it, slipping away into the fog. In the same moment, with a slow, cracking sound, the lamp beside her flickered out.

Friendship

ALEX ONCE TOLD SONJA A STORY about two bears that lived in a far-off land. He couldn't remember where he'd heard it. The story made Sonja cry even though Alex claimed it was a happy story. When he told it they were lying in bed and it was late at night and neither of them could sleep.

The bears were kept in an enclosure outside of a factory. Perhaps as entertainment for the workers, a distraction, though no one could really remember. The workers believed the bears were brothers. The enclosure held old stumps, a trough of water, and a variety of things for the bears to bite and scratch.

The bears were not brothers. They were not related at all. And this was not their only secret.

They liked each other. They liked the lunch break, too, when the workers came out and smoked cigarettes and held sandwiches between the fence's electrical wires. The bears sometimes shocked their noses and leapt back, surprised, with a whoof. The workers laughed; the bears shook their heads for a moment, then leaned toward the sandwiches again.

One day the workers no longer appeared. The man who fed the bears also went missing. The bears waited. They grew thin, and drank from the muddy puddle. They waited, hoping to be discovered.

The bears had been very careful not to let anyone know this fact: one of them could not see. He was blind, and so his friend guided him, grunted and nudged him toward the food, herded him away from the electric fence. This did not change, after they'd been abandoned. The bears found grubs beneath the stumps. They barked and growled at the empty gray sky.

Once in these lonely days a great, white bear came down out of the mountains. Some would call it a polar bear, some an ice bear, some a ghost bear. This bear walked past the factory, then circled the enclosure. Grunting, he held his head low, then high, trying to understand the situation; the two bears followed—him outside the fence, them inside. And then he kept walking away until they couldn't even smell him anymore.

When the seeing bear slept, he tried to keep the blind bear against him, safe. But one morning he woke and his friend was gone. Alarmed and afraid, the seeing bear leapt about, onto the highest stump. He growled and called.

At last he saw his blind friend, beyond the wires of the fence, caught in the corner where two concrete walls met, out at the edge of the parking lot. He growled again, and his distant friend moaned and lifted his head, twisted it around as if he could see.

"The fence doesn't hurt anymore," the blind bear called. "And I've found something to eat."

These two bears were always cautious, but eventually they realized that all the people were gone from the land. So the seeing bear led the blind bear, and they lived in peoples' houses, and in grocery stores, and anywhere else they wished to live. They ate everything to be had in one place, they slept in beds and on couches, and then they moved on to the next place. Those two bears lived long lives. They never left each other as they moved from place to place.

Snowblind

THE ONLY SOUND is the whisper of the yellow jacket, her arms swinging against her sides; if she holds her arms out: silence. The snow insulates, it swallows. And there is white fog, thick, all around her.

It's possible that she's lost the right path forever. Should she feel worse about that possibility? The ground, the snowfield she crosses feels perfectly level. It neither rises nor falls. There's no wind, but the air is cold. Her eyelashes are frozen, brittle; the hairs in her nostrils feel like bristles. White, white, white. It's even possible that the ground is rolling under her, like a treadmill. She walks.

Often I think of this girl, finding her way to me—all the animals, all the travails, all the varieties of weather she must pass through.

She walks. And when the fog shifts, wiped away for a moment, there's a horizon, the sky darker than the ground. On the horizon, three shapes, three animals. Black, black and brown. She heads in that direction, she tries to keep them in sight, the fog slipping back, erasing everything, and easing away again. She is unafraid. She doesn't know what kind of person, what kind of animal, what kind of creature she is, now.

Yet when she reaches the place where the animals had been, they are gone. Footprints in the snow—hoof prints, paw prints, claw prints— but no tracks, no trail to follow.

Still, all at once there are trees, a line of trees, a forest. The snow is not so deep, beneath the branches. Snow sifts down here and there as she walks. She looks up and sees rips in the white sky, jagged windows, bright blue. This is how she knows the path has not been lost.

Beasts

NAOMI WALKED IN THE SHALLOW SNOW BENEATH THE TREES. Earlier, she had crossed a vast snowfield, through thick fog, but now blue sky showed between the jagged branches above, and in those branches birds began to sing. A bluebird was the loudest, if not the most tuneful, and it hopped from tree to tree, shaking snow loose, as if it were trying to keep Naomi's attention.

She followed the bird along a low gulley, through a thicket; the tracks of large animals marked the snow, here. Far away, then, she heard a barking, distant growling. Naomi stopped and turned a slow circle. Nothing. She stood still and listened. Nothing.

The bluebird waited, perched on a nearby branch, and then led her deeper into the forest and its shadows. Before long they came to the edge of a clearing.

Naomi paused when she saw the hut, so quiet and still with the gables of its slanted roof painted bright red. Crouching behind a fallen tree, she watched for movement, for shadows in the window; she listened for voices, for whistling. She unzipped her small pack, checking the few shreds of beef jerky left, the bag that had held nuts, the metal canteen, almost dry.

The hut stood twenty feet away, white smoke twisting from its chimney. Its walls were painted blue, up high, the same color as the sky, and then pine trees like the ones she hid beneath. Painted tree trunks, and snow, down lower, as if the hut itself had been camouflaged to blend in, not to draw notice.

Slowly, Naomi stepped into the clearing. She had to walk around to the other side to find the door, which was painted to look like a gnarled stump, round rings where it had been cut. She knocked, and waited, but there was no answer.

The door was unlocked. She turned the knob, began to push the door open; there was no voice inside, no dog barking a warning.

"Hello?" she said, then pushed the door all the way open.

It took a moment for her eyes to adjust, to take it in. The hut was all one room. A bed against one wood-paneled wall, a red blanket spread across it. A tall wardrobe. A round black woodstove, orange fire glinting in its grate, a neat pile of split firewood stacked beside it. Cupboards against the far wall, a kind of kitchen. And, closer to Naomi as she stepped inside, a long, narrow table. She closed the door, hung her coat on the doorknob.

A game of dominos had been left on the table, next to a pocket knife and a notebook with a picture of a fox on the cover. The fox stood on its hind legs in the snow, back arched, front paws ready to pounce on a mouse that was paralyzed in that moment, relieved and perplexed that the fox hadn't yet descended. Naomi opened the cover.

RULES FOR GUESTS
LEAVE THINGS AS YOU FIND THEM
DO NOT PROVOKE ANIMALS
BE RESPECTFUL WITH REGARD TO ALL CIRCUMSTANCES
CANDLES IN KITCHEN DRAWERS. MIND THEM.
WE ARE VERY HAPPY THAT YOU'RE HERE

The notebook had once been filled with the entries of guests, it seemed, but most of the pages had been torn out. What remained: two children's drawings, in blue and orange crayon—one of two dogs or bears, another of a small hand that might have been a tracing—and one page with writing on it. The comments were at once cryptic and superficial, and even the most recent dates were old, from almost ten years before:

A better time than anticipated!
A few arguments, tho perhaps they were necessary ones.
It's a little like being inside a fairytale.

We'd been forewarned about the bears and the rest of the animals,
and will in time feel fortunate for the experience. We slept so soundly!
Within days our clocks were all turned around and we were
sleeping all day, awake all night when of course we couldn't
go outside at all. Still, we entertained ourselves, whittling
and playing word games. The muesli left behind was tremendous.

Directions were appallingly bad. If it's true that this stretch of country
can be reclaimed, communication must improve.

In the kitchen, she found the candles. She also found a loaf of bread and a plate of butter, a pitcher of water, seven eggs in a metal basket. At the far end of the counter, a pineapple—she almost didn't recognize what it was, at first. Pulling a cast iron pan from a hook, she set it on the woodstove, scooped some butter in, then cracked three eggs into the hot pan, eating them half-cooked, almost burning her chest as she leaned over the woodstove. She ate bread. She drank straight from the pitcher. White snow shone in through the windows.

If she left now, where would she go? She pulled out the bench and sat at the table, trying to cut into the pineapple with the dull pocket-knife, knowing that the longer she waited the more likely it was that someone—whoever had kindled the fire—would return.

When she went outside to wash her hands in the snow, Naomi squinted into the darkness beneath the trees. Next, she walked slowly around the hut. The only footprints in the snow were her own.

Back inside, she ate another piece of bread with butter, then sat at the table, pulled the pen from the notebook's binding and began to write on a blank page in the back:

I don't know where I am or where I'm going. I'm tired. I was on a ship and in the middle of the night put off in this place. My grandmother died, and what I'm doing was in her will, or she planned for it, but now I think it could have gone wrong. I miss her, and I miss my friends. I wish I knew when it was the last time I'll ever see someone. Maybe we should always say goodbye as if it might be. We should never part without telling a person how we feel. The will said I am supposed to help someone. Could that be right? First I'd have to find them, and right now I feel like I'm the one who could use some help.

Naomi tore out this page. Standing, she fed it into the woodstove, added a couple more logs on top of it. She was hot, sweating; she stripped off her sweater, her boots and socks, her snowpants, until she wore only a t-shirt, her black leggings. Outside, it grew darker. Lighting candles along the table, she began to write again. This time she did not try to explain or account for herself. Instead, she wrote a story about a dog, a story her friend Sonja had once told her. Writing the story made her think of Sonja in a way that made Naomi miss her, but also made her feel less alone.

The shadows gathered, flickered along the wall. They seemed to breathe. Now the window reflected back. The candles' flames, the fire in the stove, her pale face. There were a few plates and cups in the kitchen, but most of the cupboards and shelves were empty. In one drawer, a piece of butterscotch candy; Naomi sucked it as she looked around, pausing every now and then to listen. Silence.

She opened the tall wardrobe last, its door sticking and whining open. Inside, a shifting sound, a rustle of black fur.

An animal spilled out, tumbled after her.

She leapt back, her hands in front of her face.

No claws scratched her skin, no fangs bit and slashed at her. She brought her hands down, opened her eyes. It was a long, black fur coat, fallen from its hanger in the wardrobe. Stepping closer, she lifted the heavy coat and saw what it had been covering: a blue suitcase that looked like her suitcase, the one she had left behind, in her cabin on the ship. She pulled it out, set it on the bed, opened it. Her clothes, her camera—all the things she'd packed for her journey, along with the copy of *Watership Down* from the ship's library. Somehow all these things, here, following her or sent ahead to await her arrival.

Naomi spread them out, folded them, packed them as they'd been. Then, exhausted, she stretched out across the bed. Half-asleep, eyes closed, drifted off, she suddenly felt someone else, that she was not alone in the room. She opened her eyes; there was no one else there. She was alone, but someone had been there, watching her. And now she heard roaring, growling—beasts far out in the night, in the forest, all the darkness surrounding the hut. What was she supposed to do about that?

After a time, there was silence again, the feeling of these dark trees holding their branches taut, holding a space around the hut. Naomi waited, she listened; without meaning to, she drifted off to sleep.

Cairns

It is said that animals persist in this land. They stay in the shadows during the day; they're wily and hardy, difficult to witness. The elephants, the bears, the wild dogs. They're so cautious! They live in the ruins, all the empty spaces that the people have left behind.

You walk away from where you slept last night and the eggshells you drop are invisible against the white snow. Soon there will be no snow, no trees to cast shadows. Hardboiled eggs give you the strength you'll need.

When a person dies, can no one recall the sound of that person's voice?

There are no birds, no animals, the trees sparser overhead. Over a ridge, and suddenly a vast valley spreads out below. The valley floor is pocked by darker circles, clumps of sagebrush. A long, curved road, slightly paler than the land around it, cuts the valley in two.

To the right, then, something glints—down below, perhaps half a mile away. And then another flash of light. Four squares, as if mirrors had been set there on the valley floor, reflecting upward. Signals.

———

You take off your snow pants and tie them, along with your jacket, to the outside of your pack; your shadow slides along, a dark octopus beside you.

You believe you're here to help someone, yet there is no one to be found. And what would it mean to help someone, to lend assistance? What skills and strengths does a girl like you possess? You're a good listener, a solid friend, you are not easily frightened.

———

Goats are also extremely hardy animals. They'll eat the wicker seat of a rocking chair or contend with laundry hung from a line. They are capable of standing on their hind legs and balancing on the precarious faces of cliffs. The pupils in their intelligent eyes are rectangular.

———

Along the slope, jagged black stones have been piled into cairns. As if making a trail, a way down to the valley. You reach out your hands as you pass, brushing their sharp edges. A flash of white, then, between the dark stones. You stop, you dig it out, this ball of white, brittle paper. As you pick it up, it begins to come apart, into these shreds, these scraps with writing on them. They fall, blown by the wind, and you stamp your foot atop them before they can get away. You gather the scraps, weight them with stones.

You read them, you read this, and once each has been read you fold it tight and put it in your pocket.

Perhaps these fragments are part of something larger, something that makes perfect sense, a coherent whole, another kind of trail. Perhaps this is all there is. In any case, these scraps of paper were brought together for a reason, hidden here to be found.

There are times when there's nothing sweeter than a drink of cool water.

———

You cut back and forth between the sagebrush on the valley floor, unable to walk straight to where you're going. The wind comes warm, gritty, and it's difficult to see where the mirrors were now that you are no longer on the ridge or the slope. You turn and look at the black cairns, then keep moving toward where you think those reflections were.

You have no shadow, now. It is somewhere else, doing whatever it wants to do.

You approach a low wash, a kind of gully; closer, you understand that the flashing square shapes are the tops of cars that have been swallowed up, buried in sagebrush and tumbleweeds. The paint has been scorched from the exposed surfaces, the colors dull along the sides. You are fifty feet from the road, now. Setting down your pack, you wade through the dry, spiny tumbleweeds, trying to reach the nearest car. A pale golden sedan.

Closer, you realize that the driver's side door is ajar, the window open. You lift tumbleweeds out of the way, throw them aside. The metal is almost too hot to touch, and it isn't only that the vehicles are surrounded—the tumbleweeds are also inside the cars, filling them entirely. You imagine the sharpness, the feeling of sitting in a car like this, so crowded, pinned by spines, and in that moment you also imagine the skeletons that might be beneath the tumbleweeds, hidden, sitting and waiting here, unable to move.

———

Space pushes on your body, the emptiness vast in every direction. This is exactly how your body can be crushed by the pressure, the thick wind at the bottom of the ocean.

———

The road is smoother from a distance than up close. Walking on it, it's all jagged rocks underfoot, the twisting trails of snakes in the sand. There are no tracks of vehicles.

Black shadows slide smoothly along the ground. When you look up, there are no birds in the sky.

———

Later, the sun is gone and as the sky darkens the stars rise up. There are so many of them, thick around you as you walk. The stars remind you of another time, a night when you went camping with two of your friends. You drove and drove through a desert, washed out canyons looking like the rivers they once were, stars everywhere. You weren't certain where you were or where you were going, but with friends that's not always a painful uncertainty.

———

Some believe that restlessness does not possess a negative or positive connotation. Like most things, it's a matter of how you put it into practice.

———

The three of you shared a tent, the sound of zippers' teeth, whispers that died down into sleep.

In the night you awakened, your bladder full. Quietly, so quietly, careful not to wake your friends, you crept out alone under the stars, the ground almost frozen beneath your bare feet. You pulled down your long underwear, squatted behind the parked truck, one hand on its cold metal door to steady yourself.

Starting back to the tent, you saw four brighter stars, low on the horizon, trembling and jostling back and forth against the darkness. Your friends—you recognized their black silhouettes. The bright round lamps on their foreheads blinded you, the flashlights in their hands.

You said you thought they were in the tent, asleep. They didn't say where they'd been. You didn't ask; you just followed them into the tent, slipped into your warm sleeping bag. One headlamp was still on, shining up from the tent floor as you all got comfortable. You imagined how it might look from outside, your three shadowy shapes, your round heads, your arms stretching across each other.

———

The next morning: the tent trembling in the dark wind, the smoking coals of the campfire that has almost burned itself out.

Please Don't Worry

ALEX STRETCHES OUT ON THE BED, one finger following a crack in the flowered wallpaper. He's been staying here in Naomi's grandmother's house for almost three weeks. He's watching over things, and it still doesn't feel right: a dead lady's house, her granddaughter far away.

The sky is dark blue out the window, though the sun's gone down and the streetlights are coming on. Alex is listening to Sonja, who's taking a shower in the bathroom across the hall. Singing a song, her words broken up by the slap of the water against the tile.

Sonja's t-shirt lies twisted on the floor in the hallway. Closer, her jeans, collapsed in on themselves, her pale blue underwear nestled inside. Her canvas bag leans against the wall.

Rolling over, Alex grabs one handle, drags the bag toward him. Inside: a green toothbrush; a bottle of water; her phone and wallet; a book, *Watership Down*; a brown bag containing half a bagel—he takes a bite, returns it—and a manila envelope, addressed to Sonja.

The envelope is ripped, scuffed, the stamps torn off, the return address smeared away. It's flat, but it's heavy, and the seal is broken. Alex sits up on the bed, undoes the envelope's metal clasp.

The first photograph is of Naomi, her black hair blowing all around her, blue water behind her, a white railing. This must be on the ship—Alex remembers the day she left, wearing the same gray sweater, the same brown tights. She's not looking at the camera.

The next picture is of two polar bears, and then one of a field of snow, some animals in the distance. The last one shows an old man on a beach, standing in front of some kind of hut. The old man's holding out a hand, as if to say hello, and he wears a plaid shirt. His other hand tugs on his long, raggedy beard, a gray that's almost white.

Inside the envelope there's also folded paper with writing on it. A letter. Alex pauses for a moment, listens—still the slap of water, still Sonja singing from across the hall—and then he unfolds the paper and begins to read:

Well S, they just gave me your letter, three days since I saw you, three days since I left. Did you give it to someone on the ship? I don't know why it took so long, but I hardly understand how anything works, here. I like that you wrote the letter while I was asleep, next to you in bed. I wonder if I heard the scratching in my dreams and I already got your letter that way, my mind understanding the shapes of the letters like that game where you trace them on my back? It did seem kind of familiar to me!

Anyway, it's funny to think of Alex sleeping in that bed, or staying in my grandmother's house. I wonder what the two of you are doing. You say that you've always been afraid of the house. Why? Maybe you weren't being serious.

I wonder about Alex, the two of you. I miss you, too. And yes we'll do all the same things when I come back. Whenever that is. No one tells me anything! In fact, only one person tells me anything. His name is Joachim and he says he's the only person who speaks English on this ship. I doubt it, but they don't really let me move around very much. I'm actually the only passenger, or that's what Joachim says, and you've seen how big this thing is.

The last two days it's just been blue in every direction. No land, no other boats, nothing.

I keep thinking of that story you told me about how when you were a girl you tried to make plants grow with your mind, standing next to them with your eyes closed and thinking it, opening your eyes and believing it. I want to believe that, too. I want to believe in a lot of things because so much of what's supposed to make sense doesn't make sense to me.

This Joachim—he uses the word "certainly" all the time. He's thin and small and has this perfect beard and won't tell me where he's from, or really anything. I like him. He's entertaining, and frustrating, but I can't decide if he's making any decisions.

He did tell me he sees things in the dark ocean at night, and something about fires that made no sense. I think he's lonely. But isn't everyone always a little bit lonely? I miss you. I miss the way your skin smells in the morning and the way you'd swim in your sleep, dreaming. I miss being kicked by you! I pretend at night that you are sleeping beside me. And then I wake up and there's just all the ocean framed by my window.

Yes, I do remember the time we hid in my little brother's closet. How could I forget that?

Will you check on him, if you see him? The night before I left he told me he's been going out at night and walking on rooftops, just getting up on top of peoples' houses to see what he can see and hear. I told you how he comes home so late already and the girl he hangs out with, the one with the snake.

I miss you a lot. I keep thinking how much better it would be if you were here with me now in this bed. I'd read this book to you, all about these rabbits.

Here, the handwriting changes. From Naomi's cursive sprawl to tighter, more controlled letters and words, clearly written by someone else. The ink is darker, as if the pen had been pushed into the paper with greater force.

I hope you miss me also. It would be a positive emotion to know that. Don't forget me and I won't forget you, and in time I will return and we will resume all of our activities. Please don't worry about me, as Joachim is remarkably able and has my best interests and safety in the forefront of his mind. Whether there is foul weather or pirates or a mutiny, whether there are beings existing in the dark water who might be called bears, all will be well and I will remain your true friend.

Yours sincerely, Naomi

Alex reads the last part over again, then folds the paper and slides it back into the manila envelope with the photographs. He returns it all to Sonja's bag, then pushes the bag against the wall, just the way it had been. The water has stopped running, now; he can hear her in the bathroom, her feet on the tile, then coming across the hallway.

"You're still in bed?" she says.

"Obviously."

"I thought we were going to eat something." Sonja tosses her towel on the bed, then steps closer to the mirror that's propped against the wall.

Alex watches as she combs her wet hair. She tilts her head one way, then the other. She's tall and slender; her hair's lighter, when it's dry, but it looks dark now. Water drips down her bare back.

"It'll be different," he says, "when Naomi comes back."

"What do you mean?"

The house creaks, a cracking sound overhead. They both look up at the ceiling.

"I don't know," he says. "It's harder to talk to you when you're naked."

"Close your eyes, if it's so distracting."

Sonja's wet footprints shine, catching the streetlights' glare through the window. The bedroom is on the second floor, and someone outside might be able to see her.

"Will you tell me something?" he says.

"Probably."

"When you were a girl, did you really think you could make plants grow just by thinking about it?"

"It wasn't that simple. I had to close my eyes, and think really hard. Did I tell you that?"

Alex rolls over, his head now at the foot of the bed. He reaches out, but can't quite reach her. The dimples at the small of her back, the vertebrae of her spine. In the mirror he can see her watching him, and then she looks away, at her own reflection again.

"I read Naomi's letter," he says. "The one she wrote you."

Sonja turns and sits on the corner of the bed, her hip against his shoulder. She's still combing her hair; drops of water fall cold on his face, his neck.

"I wanted you to read it," she says. "I knew you would."

"That end part," he says. "Naomi didn't write that. About the pirates, the bears."

"Obviously."

"And?" he says.

"And what?"

"What do you think is happening? I mean—"

"Whatever it is, there's nothing we can do about it," she says. "Can we talk about something else?"

Alex nods, but he doesn't know what to say. He trails his finger around her shoulder blades, down the knobs of her spine.

"Will you read to me?" Sonja pulls her bag across the floor; she takes out the book, hands it to him, then lies back so their bare shoulders touch. She closes her eyes to listen.

Alex takes out the bookmark and begins to read: "'Fiver sat trembling and crying among the nettles as Hazel tried to reassure him and to find out what it could be that had suddenly driven him beside himself. If he was terrified, why did he not run for safety, as any sensible rabbit would? But Fiver could not explain and only grew more and more distressed.'"

"Keep reading," Sonja says, when Alex pauses.

"I thought you were hungry."

"Not anymore," she says. "Right now I want to see what happens with these rabbits. When you read, Naomi could be reading it, at the same time. You see? It's like we're together."

"The three of us?"

"Not exactly," she says. "I mean I'm with you, and at the same time I'm with her. Now, read."

The Hill

A GIRL HAD BEEN WALKING across a flat desert for several days, so she was delighted to see a round hillside ahead. Something to climb, some variation. A white path switched back and forth across the hill, through dark green plants with small, white flowers. The green was so dark it was almost black; shadows shifted inside the plants as she climbed.

The girl had come a long way and had not lost hope. Her grandmother had sent her on a journey to help someone. Around her, a buzzing came and went. A rustling of the plants, hidden snakes, a quiver in the air.

Among the plants there came to be piles of sharp black stones as tall as the girl. The stones were the size of a man's head, and jagged; the wind blew through them and it sounded like voices, whistling voices that the girl could not understand.

She stood still for a moment, considering whether to take one of the piles of stones apart, to see if there was anything inside. Just then, all the way at the top of the hill, where it cut against the sky, something moved. A small, round shape, moving back and forth along the line of the horizon. It looked as if one of the stones had come loose from its pile and had figured out how to move on its own.

The girl resumed walking, and as she did she realized that the round shape—swaying, rising, now—was a head, the head of another person, someone climbing up the other side of the hill, toward her. Next, a long neck became visible, and narrow shoulders, a thin arm rising up to wave.

It appeared to be a man. The light shone behind him, so it was difficult to see his face as he approached. He was a young man, so thin, with a large Adam's apple that trembled as he stopped before her, both of them standing close together on the white path.

"Hello!" he said.

She stepped aside. For some reason she had not expected him to speak.

"I don't know you," he said to her. "I thought I might know you."

He wore a black suit that was hopelessly wet, dripping onto the white path. His pale skin was also wet. When he took off his sunglasses, the girl realized they were made from the pieces of highway reflectors, orange, connected with string.

"I've been sent to help someone," she said. "Is it you?"

"I don't reckon so," he said.

"What are all these piles of stones?" she said.

"Someone must have stacked them up, here," he said. "I agree." He glanced past her, down into the flatlands, allowing the silence to grow. Finally, he spoke again, more softly now: "It'd help me to hear where you've been, what you've seen."

"Some empty buildings," she said. "Broken cars, out in the desert. Bears and other animals. I read about them, but I never saw any. Snow."

"Sounds perfect," he said, smiling and beginning to move around her, fitting his sunglasses back over his eyes. "I'm probably heading in the right direction, then."

The girl stepped aside, then turned to watch him as he walked away, down the curving white path. She called after him.

"Have you seen any snakes?"

"Absolutely," he said, turning to face her. "This whole country's thick with snakes."

"Poisonous?"

"Haven't tried to find out!" The man laughed, and waved as he turned, resuming his descent.

The girl reached the top of the hill a little while later. She looked out over the vast, blue sea, far below. It stretched in every direction, lined with rows of waves. No islands or whales spouting or ships to be seen. She began down the switchbacks toward the sea; soon she could hear the sound of the waves as they slapped the shore. Soon seagulls hovered overhead.

Before long, the girl also saw a structure on the beach, a kind of shack. The path led straight to it. And in front of this shack, two dark shapes slid back and forth, their bodies trembling in the heat of the sun. Closer, she realized it was two animals, their shadows making them look twice as large as they were, and stranger.

The two animals appeared to be bears. The way they paced, facing her, the girl could tell that they'd seen her coming and were waiting for her, anticipating her arrival.

If a Person Is About to Touch You

IF A PERSON IS ABOUT TO TOUCH YOU, you can already feel it. If you are about to meet someone, your body may already know it, a tremor in your organs. If a hand hovers over your bare skin, you can sense its presence. That's the simple, invisible way a hand can convey its intentions—which are, after all, a kind of thinking. Hands have brains, and hearts. Every finger does. This can be proved by the delay, the time it takes to understand what our hands have done, and why. Hands! They are the vehicles of intuition. When I am beset by emotion, when I think of something, that's when I ask my hands for assistance. And then when my hands suddenly do something, that is the time for me to react. They're out in front of me—they're almost always in front of me, in my field of vision, the part of myself that I know best. When I see my face in a mirror, I am often startled, or disappointed. My hands would never surprise me like that. I recognize them, reaching out for you.

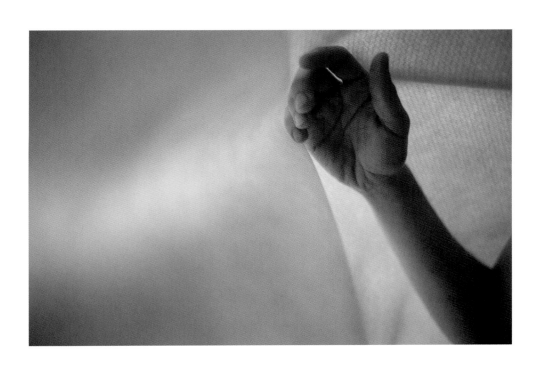

The Granddaughter
and the Grandfather

ONCE A GIRL TRAVELED DOWN A STEEP, WINDING PATH which led to the sea. A ragged hut was set up on the beach, and before it two large black dogs ranged. As the girl approached, they barked at her, sharp tails cutting the air, stiff legs angling back and forth. It seemed their voices were the crashing of waves, that the dogs held the sea inside them, for the noise of their barking was drowned.

"Hello," the girl said. "I mean no harm." She held up her hands, realizing that if she could not hear the dogs, they could not hear her. She moved closer, careful not to look them in the eyes.

The hut appeared to be made of wood that had floated in from the sea. Walls of scrap metal, where there were walls, a roof of palm fronds. Stones had been set into a crumbly foundation.

"Hello?" the girl said, stepping inside.

Papers and photographs, weighted down with stones, covered one low table. Hammers and saws hung from nails, ropes strung here and there, through heavy wooden pulleys. A bucket of water—she almost drank from it, then saw the three fish, just longer than her hand, swimming inside it. She checked behind her; the dogs stood ten feet away, silently watching. In that moment she realized that some of the ropes were in fact snakes, dead snakes, hung from their tails, heads hanging down as if to bite anyone who passed beneath them. The girl drank the last of the water in her canteen as she stepped through the hut, through an open wall, around a corner.

An old grandfather sat there, cross-legged, his eyes closed. The grandfather had a long, gray and white beard, bare feet, tattered clothing. A plaid shirt, black trousers. She could not tell if he was resting, or asleep, or even if he was alive. The clatter of the waves covered her approach. Closer, she saw that he was breathing, his body rising and falling with the sound of the waves.

The grandfather's eyes were bright, sharp blue when they eased open. He smiled, and held out his hands, as if to embrace the girl.

"I came down the path," she said. "I'm on a journey and I'm traveling through this land."

"Do I know you?" he said. "You seem familiar to me."

The grandfather stood and stretched his old, thin body. He rubbed his arms and legs as if to wake them, and then he laughed. When he laughed, he tipped his face to the sky, his hands on his hips.

"I'm glad you've come," he said, "everything seems familiar to me, and eventually I figure it out, all the things and people and how I know them."

"I've come from a far-off place," she said.

"So have I," said the grandfather. "I'll tell you the story of how I came to be here." He paused, tugged at his beard. "Are you here to hurt or help me?"

"I believe I'm here for a reason," she said.

"We'll be friends," he said. "Here, come inside. You must be hungry?"

The two black dogs now lay on woven mats in the hut. They raised their heavy heads, snapping their jaws and licking their snouts, when they saw the grandfather. He stroked their heads and they settled down, tails sweeping along the stone floor.

He turned to the girl, squinted. "Are you really a person?" he said.

"Yes."

"Have you heard the story," he said, "of the girl with the shadow of a bear?"

"No."

"Or the one who found a whale bone and rubbed it all over her body? Who married a whale?"

"I don't know."

"You're not that kind of girl," he said, "are you?"

"No," she said. "I don't plan to marry a whale."

"Good," the grandfather said. "Remind me if I forget that. I am a forgetful man."

He pulled over a stump for the girl to sit on, then settled near her on the floor.

"Would you believe me," he said, "if I told you that one day I simply swam out of this sea? I pulled myself up here on this beach. That's how I was born."

"You were a baby?"

"Listen!" he said. "Girl. No, no, no. I was not a baby. I was a man when I was born, the same as I am a man now. This is not so long ago I'm talking about. And I was already forgetful, I knew so little, and yet I was fortunate. Here—" He spread out his arms, waving them around. "—Right on this spot I found a pile of clothing—this clothing—and it fit me. So that was the beginning."

"Now I remember the story of the whale's wife," she said. "And her friend, who found the eagle bone—"

"That was not far from here," the grandfather said. "Are you that kind of girl?"

"No," she said.

"In those early days," he said, slapping his shirt pockets, taking out a pair of eyeglasses and putting them on, "I found my glasses—I hadn't realized how clouded my vision had been!—and then it was easier to find my other things, hidden for me in the gaps between the stones."

As the grandfather spoke, the girl looked around his hut. At the row of colored glass bottles, brushed by the sea, the stacks of abalone shells. The hanging snakes, the thick ropes and cracked wooden pulleys, all strung up. The chest with its drawers marked HOOKS and KNIVES and STRING. The grandfather held up a book now, opening it, so she could read the title—*The Martian Chronicles*—on the spine.

"Even my books were here," he said. "After a time I came to remember them. And this one, here, my name was written in the front. Oscar. I came to remember that. So then I had my name again." Smiling, he set the book aside and lifted a stone from the table, began sifting through the photographs there. "Do you think," he said, "might you be my granddaughter? You're feeling more familiar to me."

"I don't think so," she said. "My one grandfather died when I was very young; I hardly remember him at all. The other one is still alive, and he's not you. Do you have any water?"

The grandfather nodded, then stood and walked out of the hut. In a moment he returned with a metal pail, a steel dipper rattling against the side. The girl drank.

"And the dogs?" she said. "Were they here when you swam in from the sea?"

"No," he said, leaning to pat the closer dog. "The hounds came later.

They came over the hill and down the path, just as you did. And now you've come to do me a favor."

"A favor is something to be requested," the girl said. "One can't simply tell a person that she's going to do a favor."

"Tomorrow," he said. "We'll get to that tomorrow, after we've eaten and slept." Now he snatched up one photograph, flashing it at her, then another, and another. A man with birds fluttering around him; a naked man with a black mustache, riding a horse in the snow; a bald man swimming in a dirty pool. "These are all me," the grandfather said. "I didn't recognize myself, at first, but if I look at them long enough—"

"They don't look like you," the girl said. "You said that you swam out of the sea, and you were born a man, that you didn't remember, that you're forgetful."

The grandfather gently shook his head, still looking at the photographs in his hands. "I was younger," he said, "in other times and places. I was a handsome man, having these adventures. I have always delighted in the weather."

When the grandfather and the girl left the hut, the waves were louder. The grandfather started a fire in a circle of stones, behind a windbreak, and began to bring out pots and pans, to take the knives from their drawer.

That evening he and the girl ate a stew of fish and clams and snake. She looked up from her bowl; the two black dogs licked the pots and then chased each other up and down the dark beach. The tide was ebbing, now, the moon rising, the waves further away.

———

.

THE GRANDDAUGHTER AND THE GRANDFATHER

The girl could not sleep. Perhaps it was the scratchiness of the wool blankets, or the dogs so nearby on the floor of the hut. She could not hear the grandfather's snores, but watched his dark body as it rose and fell. She heard the waves, and the rustle of the dried palm fronds of the roof, lifting in the wind. She heard the knives in the knife drawer, sharpening each other, having their conversations. The girl did not sleep, but she dreamed that in the night her head was traded for one of the dog's heads, and the other dog switched heads with the old man. That dog would hold its head high, to keep its long beard from dragging on the ground.

———

In the morning, the dogs stand and stretch—hunching their backs, sticking one hind leg out at a time—then walk out toward the sea. They sniff the air, they feel the light all around them.

The girl, her name is Naomi, is already awake. She lies still and watches the dogs go. She has not slept, and her body feels snarled, unpredictable.

The old man is still sleeping. He sleeps with his arms over his head, his weathered palms facing up, his grand white beard spread across his chest in five tangled points. Standing over him, Naomi cannot see his throat. She gathers ropes and straps—there are so many hanging around the hut, as if brought here for this purpose.

Careful not to wake him, she binds his wrists, his ankles. She ties him to the thick supports of the hut, knotting and double-knotting so he will be unable to free himself.

Next, she walks out of the hut, down the slope of the shore, and into the sea. The waves knock her back, at first, breaking over her knees, her thighs, but she goes deeper, letting the current pull her out further.

She dives down, deep underwater. She tastes salt, holds her breath, hands scrabbling against the sand and stone and shells. She believes this might take her to another place, even deliver her home, yet every time she surfaces she is in the same place—the tall, dark hill, the rickety hut with the old man bound inside, the two silent dogs on the shore, watching her. She goes under again.

This time her hands can't find the bottom. She's deeper, and the current twists her body above her, and around her dark shadows fold closer, ease away. Seals, or underwater animals, darknesses reaching out. And then there's a new sound, traveling through the thick water, a ticking, a mechanical whir. Surfacing, she faces away from the shore, out to sea.

There, on the horizon: the long, dark silhouette of a ship.

In the same moment, she's pulled under again, cut on her neck, her shoulder, caught from behind. It's the dogs, both of them, still barking without any sound, their front legs reaching out, claws raking her skin. They won't stay back, she's choking, they'll drown her, and so she kicks free, into the waves as they follow.

She struggles back into shore, crawling as the waves pull at her, still coughing. The dogs are bounding all around her in the shallows, happy—they've saved her!—and the old man is standing here, ropes and straps trailing from his wrists and ankles.

"I thought you'd stop me," she says. "I thought—"

"About that favor," he says.

Naomi follows the old man back to his hut. He undoes the knots at his wrists as he walks, gathering the ropes in his hands, chuckling to himself. At the hut, he goes straight to the table and begins shuffling through the photographs again.

"It was a good sleep," he says. "So helpful. I remember more, now. Do I remember you? I'm not certain, I truly am not, but I was right about why you're here. I can feel that."

You can slip away, you can take a risk. Be decisive.

Turning, he begins to adjust the pulleys, the heavy ropes stretched across the hut's open side. Naomi sees a wire that she hadn't noticed before, thin and sharp, tied to ropes that are strung between blocks and pulleys, that wind around a metal spool, a rusted crank with a handle sticking out one side. Next the old man twists the wire so it is a circle, its edges pulling in opposite directions. He bends down and puts his head through this circle, his head resting on a table. His face is turned toward her.

"This is the thing," he says. "You'll turn that handle there, that crank. And then we're done."

Naomi steps closer. She touches the handle.

"I don't know," she says.

"You can look away," he says, you can close your eyes. Hurry. I can't bend down like this all day."

Naomi closes her eyes.

"To kill a person who's already dead," he says, "that is the kindest thing of all."

She begins to turn the crank.

"Wrong way," he says.

She reverses direction. The crank spins freely, then catches—the pulleys squeak, but they are doing their job; it's like tightening a nut, and then the bolt is broken and the ropes go slack and the sound is not what she expected.

It's the body that falls, legs kicking, feet slapping, hands slapping the stone floor, the red blood pumping out at the neck, a puddle seeping toward Naomi's feet. Her eyes are open.

She steps out from under the hut, toward the water, scans the horizon. The ship is nowhere to be seen. The old man's eyeglasses clatter loose, on the stones; his head swings from her hand, she doesn't know how or when she picked it up, but now she holds it from its bristly beard.

She looks back, once, almost expecting the headless body to follow, to jerk stiffly after her, spilling blood from its neck; yet the body remains where it was, collapsed on the floor of the hut. What she sees is the black dogs, running away—away from the hut and up the path, climbing the dark hill. Their black shapes move up the switchbacks of the white path like marbles in a maze, climbing until they reach the top and go over, gone.

"I knew you were smart," the old man says. "I knew you were clever."

She almost drops the head. It rises and falls as he speaks, his beard jerks in her fingers. His sharp blue eyes are wide open. Blood runs red down the side of his face. The tip of his tongue pokes out through bloody teeth.

"I knew you would see what had to be done," he says. "You're smart. Thank you. Not everyone would see. I feel so wonderful, so much lighter."

"Enough," she says, glancing down for only a second. "You're supposed to stop talking. There are no more things to say."

"Exactly," the head says. "Isn't it grand?"

Naomi runs out toward the water, up to her knees in the waves. She swings the head as hard as she can, around and around, then lets go of the beard.

The head disappears for a moment, then surfaces, bobbing on the waves. It sputters and chokes, still shouting.

"Thank you! Thank you! Thank you!"

The waves bring the head in closer, and then the current takes hold and pulls it away, at an angle, farther and farther from shore. Before long, Naomi can no longer see the head, but she can still hear him.

She never tells anyone what happened, in all the years that are to follow. She never forgets the sound of the old man's voice, his gratitude rising from the waves.

AUDIO, VIDEO, INTERVIEWS:
WWW.SPELLSPROJECT.COM

SOPHIA BORAZANIAN

is a photographer living and working in New Orleans. After attending Ohio State University to study photojournalism, she moved south to document her life in Louisiana. Inspired by the Art Deco architecture of her hometown of Cleveland, Ohio, she is now making large collages of her images for murals on buildings throughout the city of New Orleans.

SARA LAFLEUR-VETTER

is a multimedia journalist with a passion for telling stories of the underdog and the underbelly of society. She holds a Master's in Journalism specializing in documentary film from the Berkeley Graduate School of Journalism. She believes in the power of film and photography, she's engaged to a wonderful man named Leaf, and she hopes to live long enough to tell good stories.

The Human Heart, Uganda
2009

Birdman, Italy
2001

Call of the Wild, Pennsylvania, USA
2009

Tea Time, Egypt
2010

Hello, I'm Dreaming, Dahab, Egypt
2008

Ass Backwards, Dahab, Egypt
2008

White Desert Sky
2012

Old Man and the Sea, Dahab, Egypt
2012

Old Man and the Sea, Dahab, Egypt
2012

PETER EARL McCOLLOUGH is a photographer and filmmaker based in the San Francisco Bay Area.

SHAENA MALLETT

is a documentary storyteller, teacher, gardener, and seeker of things deep and true. She practices permaculture, herbalism, and currently resides in North Carolina.

Wolves Running Forever
2007

Feast of the First Morning of the First Day
2012

Twilight
2012

How the Light Gets In
2010

Harbor
2008

Sunrise
2009

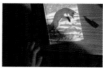

Signs of Life
2009

Little One
2010

Seafoam
2008

Clementine
2011

COLLEEN PLUMB

makes photographs and videos that look at ambivalence and contradiction in our relationships with non-human animals. Her work is held in several permanent collections and has been widely published and exhibited. Her first monograph is *Animals Are Outside Today* (Radius Books, 2011). Plumb teaches in the Photography Department at Columbia College Chicago and lives in Chicago with her husband and their two fierce daughters.

Pool Trees
2003

Ruth with Paperwhites
2011

Burying Jack II
2009

Winter Park
2000

Polar Bears with Audience
2009

Ruth on Garage
2011

Trunk with Hand
2006

Horse Horizon
1998

ACKNOWLEDGMENTS

Sophie, Sara, Peter, Shaena, Colleen. A person couldn't ask for more talented, generous, trusting, game collaborators. Thanks for saying yes right away, for your enthusiasm, and for sharing your visions.

Without the John Simon Guggenheim Memorial Foundation, this would have remained a personal project. (A debt to Andrea Barrett, Susan Choi, Stacey D'Erasmo, Adam Johnson.)

For proposing the gallery show and the huge amount of work that went into it, gratitude to Todd Tubutis, Zemie Barr, Amanda Clem and Lisa DeGrace at Blue Sky Gallery. Coordination of talent, connections, all manner of where-withal were brought by the astounding Steve Rauner at NORTH. All audio— spoken word and score—by the talented John Askew at Scenic Burrows, and with Shayla Hason and Maria Maita-Keppeler. Thank you, friends. You taught me much. Appreciation to Madelyn Villano, playing beautiful music for all those strange performances.

Immeasurable thanks to Matt Eller at Afternoon, Inc. For video design and then for book design. The way you work is an inspiration, really. Innumerable hours in service of this tormented project. The seventh collaborator, here. The beauty of the object you hold or behold, reader, is because of Matt.

A book like this is not exactly a commercial venture. Crucial support provided by the John Simon Guggenheim Memorial Foundation, Blue Sky Gallery, the Oregon Community Foundation, Stephanie Snyder and the Cooley Gallery, and the Reed College Dean's Office.

And still someone has to believe, to take a risk. Gratitude and awe to Harry Kirchner and all risk-takers at Counterpoint.

Thanks to my ingenious friends who read all or parts of this project at different times. And to Naima Karczmar-Britton for copyediting.

Grateful for the magazines and editors who first published individual pieces: "Go-Between," *Ploughshares*; "Illuminations," *ZYZZYVA*; "To Begin Is to Start," *Oregon Humanities Magazine*.

Also acknowledging the many pieces of this writing that had other sources— sometimes borrowed consciously, more often not (in which case I am oblivious to my borrowings). Whole sentences here are not mine, but have passed through me and given new context. Many folktales, and words from Emerson, Cage, Kawabata, Chekhov, etc. Thanks for your forbearance, masters.

Finally, of course: Ella, Ida, Miki.